The Twin Sheikhs

Kate Goldman

The Twin Sheikhs

Published by Kate Goldman

Copyright © 2019 by Kate Goldman

ISBN 978-1-07710-465-5

First printing, 2019

www.KateGoldmanBooks.com

PRINTED IN THE UNITED STATES OF AMERICA

Dedication

I want to dedicate this book to my beloved husband, who makes every day in my life worthwhile. Thank you for believing in me when nobody else does, giving me encouragement when I need it the most, and loving me simply for being myself.

Table of Contents

Chapter 1

"Why do handsome men always have something wrong with them?" said CJ as she burst into Blake's office. Blake was sitting at her desk looking at some work files. She looked up at her colleague and best friend CJ.

"What are you talking about?" Blake asked as she leaned back in her chair.

"It's this new client." CJ approached Blake and sat on her wooden desk.

"What is wrong with him?"

"He is handsome and rich."

"But?"

"He is so fussy! I swear there is no way of pleasing him."

Blake raised her perfectly shaped dark brown eyebrows and smiled a little. She knew what it was like to work with difficult clients.

"What does he want?" Blake asked.

"A house." CJ's brown curls bounced as she shook her head.

"That's simple enough."

"Except he rejected every sketch I have shown him. You're up next."

"What do you mean?"

"Michaela wants you on this," she said. Michaela was their boss. CJ and Blake had gone to the same university and now they were working at the same architectural company.

"Me?" Blake raised her eyebrows. CJ nodded. "Why me?"

"The client has already refused to work with four other architects before me. So Michaela asked me to call you over," said CJ.

"You should have started the conversation with that." Blake rose to her feet.

"Michaela is talking to the client right now. The client is a rich sheikh. He wants to build a house here in Austin," said CJ.

"I see, where are they now?"

"In conference room six."

"Okay." Blake straightened her black skirt.

"Good luck," CJ said to her. Blake smiled and nodded.

"Hopefully he isn't too bad."

CJ sighed. "He is so handsome and so serious. He is the type of man that would take charge." She smiled and wiggled her eyebrows. Blake laughed and shook her head. She headed for the exit. She felt curious as she headed towards the conference room. She wanted to see how handsome this sheikh was because CJ had emphasized it.

Blake reached the conference room moments later. She knocked on the thick glass door before she walked in. Her manager Michaela was sitting at the table with an unfamiliar man. He was sitting in the seat facing the door.

"Excuse me, Michaela; did you call for me?" Blake said softly.

"Yes, come in," Michaela replied. Blake nodded and walked into the room. The sheikh looked at her as she walked in.

CJ was right, Blake thought to herself. The man was wearing a crisp white shirt with two buttons unbuttoned revealing his tanned skin. The shirt hugged his bulging muscles. He had a very neat beard that did nothing to hide his strong jaw. He had dark eyebrows and a straight nose. He had dark eyes and thick eyelashes. His hair was cut neatly in a short back and sides style.

"Blake, meet Sheikh Bassem Sedarous," Michaela said to her.

"Hello, sheikh." Blake extended her hand for a handshake but the serious sheikh looked at her hand and then he looked at Michaela.

"Who is she?" His deep voice almost startled Blake. She wasn't expecting it to be so deep.

"She is one of my best architects," Michaela replied. Blake awkwardly pulled her hand back. She couldn't believe the sheikh had left her hanging like that. She pulled out a chair for herself and took a seat.

"If she is one of the best, why are you only bringing her to me now?" the sheikh asked Michaela.

"She was busy on other projects but now, one of those projects has been completed. So I believe she has some availability."

"I need the person on my case to be fully accessible to me. I do not want to work with someone that will have divided attention."

His words echoed in Blake's mind. He needed someone to be fully accessible to him only. That showed Blake that he was the type of man that did not share, and wanted things his way.

"That will not be a problem." Michaela smiled. The sheikh barely reacted. He just kept his straight face on.

"I came to you because this is one of the best architectural companies in Texas. If this architect fails to deliver something that is up to my standards, I will take my business elsewhere."

Blake raised her eyebrows. He was quite a strict and demanding man. She turned her head and looked at Michaela as she replied to the sheikh.

"I assure you that Miss Gordon is very professional and good at her job. She will do her best to give you what you want," said Michaela. The sheikh looked at Blake and sighed.

"That is what she said about the last five architects she put on this project," he said to Blake.

Blake wanted to tell him that he was probably the problem but she was not going to do that. "I can and I will deliver exactly what you need," Blake said confidently. The sheikh raised an eyebrow.

"What makes you so confident?"

"I have been successful in all my projects and have had no complaints from my previous clients."

The sheikh did not look impressed or convinced. "You look young, how long have you worked here?" he asked.

"I am twenty-six years old and I have worked here for two years," she replied.

"That is not enough experience."

"It does not mean that I am not good at my job."

"Which university did you attend?"

"MIT."

The sheikh raised his eyebrows slightly. Blake wondered if the fact that she had graduated from MIT impressed him. It was a good university, one of the best in the world. Her clients usually found it impressive.

The sheikh said nothing for a moment. He kept his gaze on Blake. He seemed to be studying her. Michaela had been watching their exchange. Her gaze had shifted back and forth between the sheikh and Blake.

"So, will you work with her?" Michaela asked.

"Sure." He did not sound enthusiastic about it at all. He rose from his seat. He was quite tall. "I do not like wasting my time. If I don't get results then I will take my business elsewhere," he added. Blake and Michaela rose to their feet.

"I will give you results," said Blake. The sheikh headed for the exit. Michaela bowed her head.

"Thank you, sheikh," she said. Blake crossed her eyebrows. Michaela straightened up and looked at Blake. "I want you to stop working on all your other projects. Give them to Cora and James," she said.

"Why would I do that?" Blake asked.

"I need your full focus on this project."

"I can handle multiple projects."

"We cannot lose him as a client. Do you know how much this would make us?"

"I don't know but I know that I don't want to give up my projects." Giving up her projects meant giving up her commission.

"Blake, forget your projects. The sheikh wants to build a massive house worth over fifteen million dollars. You will earn a lot of commission, more than all your other projects combined."

Blake raised her eyebrows. "Who is he and why can he afford to build such an expensive house?" she asked.

"Sheikh Bassem Sedarous is the crown prince of Al Huddah, and his family owns one of the largest oil companies in the world," Michaela explained.

Chapter 2

Bassem sighed as he headed out of the building. Collette Architects had a great reputation. It was one of the best architectural companies in America. The fact that the company's headquarters were located in Austin was perfect for Bassem because he wanted to build a house in Austin. His family owned oil refineries and rigs in Austin.

So far Bassem was not impressed by the service he had received. All the architects he had worked with were mediocre. They were not able to capture his vision for his house. Bassem was very meticulous. He was such a perfectionist and wanted things to be done a certain way.

The driver opened the door for Bassem as he approached the car. Bassem got into the backseat of the car and sat comfortably. The driver shut the door behind him. They drove off moments later and headed to Bassem's office. He had a meeting he needed to attend.

Blake was an attractive woman, Bassem thought to himself. She was tall, curvy and beautiful. She had long silky brunette hair, big green eyes and fair skin. However, her looks meant nothing to him. He had met women more attractive than her and all of them had the same things in common. They were shallow, opportunist and uninteresting. Bassem wondered if she was going to do a good job designing his house. He wanted something spectacular and unique.

The driver parked when they arrived at their destination. The driver got out of the car and opened the door for Bassem. The sheikh got out of the car and buttoned his suit jacket. He headed towards the entrance of the building. The glass automatic doors opened as he approached them.

"Good afternoon, Sheikh Sedarous," the receptionist greeted him as he walked into the lobby of the building.

"Afternoon," Bassem replied. He headed to the elevator and pressed the button. When the doors opened, a few staff members walked out. They all greeted the sheikh. The women greeted him with big smiles on their faces. He just nodded his head at them in acknowledgment and walked into the elevator.

Bassem headed to the conference room when he got out of the elevator. His secretary and other engineers were already there when he arrived. They all rose to their feet and bowed their heads when Bassem walked into the room.

"Good afternoon," he said. He walked over to the seat at the head of the table and pulled out his chair. "Have a seat," he said to them as he sat down. His secretary gave him a folder with information regarding their current oil rigs in Austin. Bassem's father had sent him to Austin and put him in charge of their business there because there was not much progress. Bassem's father wanted him to supervise all projects and find new clients and improve profit.

"Let's begin," Bassem ordered.

One of the geophysicists began to present his findings on one of the rigs. His job was to use mathematical models to calculate the depth of the well and estimate the well performance. When he finished, the other engineers gave Bassem progress reports.

***

"Knock, knock!" CJ said as she walked into Blake's office on Monday morning.

"Hi," Blake greeted her. Blake was tidying up her office before the sheikh's arrival.

"What are you tidying up? Your office is always so neat and tidy."

Blake smiled. "Everything has to be perfect for when the sheikh gets here. Michaela was in here five minutes ago reminding me that I should make sure that nothing goes wrong with this project," she replied.

"You are the company's last hope." CJ grinned. "No pressure," she said sarcastically. They both knew that there was a lot of pressure on Blake.

"You have designed a lot of amazing buildings. I am shocked that he did not like anything you had to offer," said Blake. She had seen a lot of CJ's work and she thought it was amazing. CJ was very talented.

CJ sighed. "He's a difficult man to please. I wish you the best of luck," she said.

"Thanks." Blake smiled. She picked up a few documents and handed them to CJ. "Michaela took me off all my other projects. She told me to give them to you and James," she said.

"Thank you. I actually wanted more projects because I am almost finished with my current one." CJ took the documents from her.

"The sheikh will be here in about ten minutes." Blake looked at the clock on the wall. It was just before 9 a.m.

"What was your first impression of him?"

Blake shrugged her shoulders. "I only spoke with him for something like two minutes. I have to meet with him once more before I have an impression of him," she replied. CJ stared at Blake with a blank facial expression.

"Well if you say so," she said. She turned on her heel and headed for the door. "I'll see you at lunch," she added.

"Bye Cora," Blake said to CJ.

A few minutes later, Tara came to Blake's office. Tara was the receptionist. She knocked on Blake's door before she walked in. "Blake, I have Sheikh Sedarous with me," she said in her high-pitched and overly friendly tone. Blake rose to her feet instantly.

"Please let him in," she said. Tara opened the door wider for the sheikh. Bassem walked into the office. He was dressed in a pair of black fitted trousers and a navy blue shirt and a pair of navy blue loafers. His body was in perfect shape. It was impressive.

"Good morning, Sheikh Sedarous," Blake greeted the sheikh as she extended her hand for a handshake. He took her hand into his and shook it firmly. He had such large and warm hands.

"Good morning, Ms. Gordon," he replied. Bassem's deep voice filled the room. It gave Blake goose bumps.

"Please have a seat." Blake gestured at the tufted chair at her desk. "Shall I get you anything to drink?"

"No, thank you," Bassem declined her offer as he sat down. Blake nodded. She walked around the desk and sat down in her chair opposite him. She opened her desk drawer and pulled out a black folder.

"This folder contains sketches and photos of my previous projects," she said as she passed the folder to Bassem. Without saying a word, Bassem took the folder and opened it. He flipped the pages as if he was looking for something specific. He barely looked at the sketches.

"I don't have much time, so I will just get to the point," he said. Blake nodded. "I have twenty acres of land and I wish to build a moderately sized home."

Moderate? There was nothing moderate about twenty acres of land, Blake thought to herself. That was a lot of land to build a house on. There were even farms smaller than that. Blake whipped out a notepad and a pen.

"I suppose you would looking to build a two-story house?" she asked. Bassem nodded.

"On the ground floor, there should be a kitchen, dining room, drawing room, library, at least two bathrooms and a coat room. I prefer wide hallways and high ceilings and a very grand entrance to the house," he said. Blake jotted down everything he said.

"Would you like to have an imperial staircase?" Blake asked.

"Yes, and it must be opposite the front door."

"Okay."

"There should be at least five bedrooms upstairs." Bassem then described the sizes he wanted the rooms to be. He was very exact about what he wanted his house to be like. It was now Blake's job to bring that dream into reality. To her it sounded simple and straightforward. However, after hearing that he had rejected everything everyone else had designed, she knew that she needed to spend a lot of time and effort designing his house. She needed to get it right. Michaela would never forgive her for losing such a great opportunity.

When they were finished, Bassem rose to his feet. "I expect to see a preliminary sketch in three days," he said. Blake raised her eyebrows. Three days was not enough time.

"Three days?" she said as she rose to her feet. She was a tall woman but not so much when compared to Bassem. He was at least five inches taller than her.

"You can't get it done by then?" he asked her.

"I can do it," she replied.

"If you have no confidence, tell me now so that we do not waste any time."

"I can do it."

Bassem slipped his hands in his pockets. "Very well then, I shall see you in three days," he said. He turned on his heel and headed out of her office.

Chapter 3

Blake had been working on the sheikh's house for two days. She didn't have much time to come up with something grand for him. She hoped that he would like her sketches because if he didn't, Michaela would blame her for losing a client. Michaela was always looking for more clients and more ways to expand their business. She was such a workaholic and a very strict manager.

Suddenly the doorbell rang. Blake rose from the sofa and rushed to the front door. She looked through the peephole to see who it was. She crossed her eyebrows when she saw that it was CJ. Blake wasn't expecting her. She opened the door.

"CJ, what are you doing here?" she asked her.

"I came to pick you up," CJ answered as she walked into Blake's apartment. She made her way to the living room. Blake shut the door and followed CJ. "I knew you would be working," CJ said while looking at the sketches Blake had been working on.

"Well, the sheikh only gave me three days. So I have to keep on working."

CJ picked up the sketches. "Wow, you did a good job with them," she said.

"Thanks, I hope he agrees." Blake sighed.

"Go get dressed."

"Why?"

"We are going out tonight." CJ smiled. She undid her trench coat and revealed a short red dress. Blake raised her eyebrows.

"You look nice. Where are you going?" She looked at CJ from head to toe. The red dress complemented her curvy figure.

"We are going to this new club called Rubies. Tonight is the opening night."

Blake laughed. "I am not going clubbing," she said.

"Oh come on! We can't miss the opening night." CJ rubbed her hands together and silently pleaded.

"We have to work tomorrow."

CJ narrowed her gaze at Blake. "You are twenty-six not forty-six. You can go out, have a good time and still make it to work tomorrow. You can survive on four hours of sleep," she said. Blake shrugged her shoulders.

"Fine. I will go and get ready," she said. She turned and left the room. She rushed upstairs and took a quick shower. When she was finished, she slipped into a thin-strapped, knee-length black dress and a pair of black high heels. She untied her hair and

16

brushed it. She walked out of her bedroom and headed back to the living room.

CJ was sitting on the sofa eating strawberries. She turned and looked at Blake as she walked into the living room. "No lipstick?" she asked.

"I didn't feel like wearing lipstick," Blake replied. CJ fished some red lipstick out of her purse and handed it to Blake.

"Put some on," she said to her. Blake shook her head as she took the lipstick from her.

"And put my strawberries back in the fridge."

"They're quite sweet." CJ put another one in her mouth. Blake shook her head. Whenever CJ came over to her apartment, she always ate her food. She even found food that Blake had forgotten about.

"Happy now?" Blake pouted her lips at CJ.

"Yes!" CJ smiled as she rose to her feet. "Let's go."

They both took their purses and left. They took a taxi to the club. When they arrived, there was a long line. There were so many people trying to get in. Blake sighed. She hated long lines.

"Don't sulk, I got our names on the guest list," CJ said to Blake.

"Really?" Blake's eyes widened.

"Of course." CJ wiggled her eyebrows. She took Blake's hand and led her to the club entrance. "Hi, our names should be on the guest list," she said to the bouncer.

"What are your names?" he asked her.

"CJ and Blake."

The tall, muscular man looked at the list. It took him a few seconds to find their names. He looked at the other bouncer and gave him a nod. The other bouncer lifted the barrier and let them in.

The club wasn't as full as Blake thought it would be. It made her feel a lot better. She hated crowded places. The interior of the club was quite sophisticated. There were nice seating areas sectioned off. The décor was interesting and beautiful. The club was different from other clubs Blake had been to.

"Let's get something to drink," CJ said. Blake nodded and followed CJ to the bar. As they were heading to the bar, Blake saw a man sitting in the VIP area with a few other men and women. She gasped when she recognized him. She yanked CJ's arm.

"Look!" she cried out in her ear. The music was a bit loud, so she had to shout.

"What?" CJ shouted back.

"It's Bassem." She pointed at the man in the wine-red long-sleeved top and black pants. CJ gasped and looked at Blake.

"It's him! Let's go say hi."

"No."

"Yes."

Blake hesitated but CJ grabbed her arm and led her towards the VIP area. Blake felt weird about running into Bassem in the club. When they reached the VIP area, Bassem looked up and made eye contact with Blake. She smiled and waved awkwardly. He waved her over. Blake climbed up the steps and then walked over to him. He gestured for her to sit down next to him.

"Hello, sheikh," Blake shouted above the music. Bassem raised his perfectly shaped eyebrows. He looked rather surprised.

"Hi," he replied.

"I did not expect to see you here."

He smiled at her. "I didn't expect to see you either," he replied. He had such a beautiful smile and he smelled good.

"I finished the preliminary sketch. I hope that you like it," she said to him.

"Let's not talk business tonight. What would you like to drink?" he asked her.

"Um, I…" Blake was confused. He seemed different from when she had met him. He looked friendlier. "I will have a lemonade," she said.

"A lemonade?" Bassem raised an eyebrow.

"I have work tomorrow."

He smiled and nodded. CJ sat down next to Blake and waved at the sheikh. He smiled at her and asked what she wanted to drink. CJ asked for a shot. She was a little more free-spirited than Blake. Bassem waved a waiter over and ordered drinks for them.

As the night progressed, Bassem and Blake engaged in conversation. She found him easy and fun to talk to. At one point, he even leaned into her and told her that she looked good. Blake smiled and thanked him.

"Would you like to dance?" Bassem asked her.

"Me?" Blake asked him. Bassem nodded. He took her hand and helped her up to her feet.

As he started dancing, Blake felt very awkward. She was not good at dancing at all. She was so stiff and had no rhythm. Bassem on the other hand was very good at dancing. He had so much rhythm.

"You're such a bad dancer," he shouted to Blake. She laughed and shrugged her shoulders. It was the truth.

Bassem was such a gentleman the entire time. He kept a respectable distance as he danced with Blake and he did not try anything inappropriate. CJ was busy downing shots and dancing with Bassem's friends. She was a much better dancer. She was having so much fun with his friends, you would think that they knew each other.

Blake and CJ ended up leaving the club after 2 a.m. Blake had come with the intention of leaving at midnight but she was having so much fun with Bassem that she had lost track of time. He had been kind and fun to be around. He ordered their drinks for them and when they were leaving, he paid their cab fare.

It had been an unexpected evening for Blake. It begun with her not wanting to go to the club but then she was glad she had gone. She had had a good time. Meeting Bassem was good. She hoped since they had broken the ice, it would make him easier to work with and that they would get along more in the future.

Chapter 4

The elevator doors opened and Blake quickly walked out. There had been an accident on her route to work which caused her to be late. She quickly approached the reception area. "Is the sheikh here?" she asked Tara.

"Yes, he is waiting in your office," Tara replied.

"Damnit," Blake muttered as she rushed to her office. She opened the door and walked into her office. Bassem was already sitting at her desk. He was looking at his phone. Blake rushed to her desk.

"Good morning, sheikh, I am so sorry I am late," she apologized. Bassem looked up from his phone.

"I do not appreciate tardiness," he said to her.

"I am not usually late. I did leave early but there was an accident. It was beyond my control."

"I do not appreciate excuses either." Bassem had such a serious facial expression. It kind of shocked Blake because when she had met him at the club, he wasn't that serious. He had been smiling at her and was so friendly.

"Noted." Blake sat down in her chair. She opened her bag and pulled out her laptop and flipped it open.

She opened the BIM software which she had used to create a 3D design of the house for the sheikh.

"Here are the designs," she said as she turned the laptop to show him. Bassem pulled the laptop closer to him and studied the designs. He took his time studying every detail. Blake could not tell what he was thinking because he kept such an expressionless face. His face gave nothing away. She wondered if he was going to like it or not.

"Did you get home too late last night?" Blake asked him. Bassem looked up from the laptop.

"No," he replied. He frowned as if he was wondering why Blake was asking him.

"Oh." Blake had left Bassem at the club and it was after 2 a.m. He had escorted Blake and CJ to get their cab and then paid for the fare. Blake was wondering what time he had gotten home.

"These designs are not bad but there is room for improvement," said Bassem.

"Okay, what would you need changing?" Blake asked him.

"The drawing room needs to be bigger. There has to be a fireplace somewhere in the room."

"Okay, I can fix that." Blake nodded. She was relieved that it was something small that she could easily adjust. She made a note of it in her notepad.

"Change the positions of the sinks in the bathrooms." Bassem leaned back in his chair. "I also don't like the location of the guest rooms. There should be a considerable distance from the master bedroom."

"For privacy purposes?" Blake smiled at Bassem but he did not return her smile. She quickly stopped smiling and just made a note of it in her notepad.

"For the master bedroom, the walk-in closet needs to be bigger," Bassem added.

Blake nodded. "I will increase the dimensions of the closet," Blake replied.

"There needs to be an annex building," said Bassem. Blake looked a little perplexed. He had not mentioned anything about an annex building before. "For staff," he added.

"I see," Blake replied.

"It does not need to be that big. I think five en-suite bedrooms, a kitchen and a living room will be enough."

Not that big? That was a very large building, Blake thought to herself. Annex buildings were usually small. Her apartment was not even that big. She lived in a two-bedroom apartment. She wanted to save up for her own house. Being an architect, she had already designed her dream house and just needed the money to realize her dream.

"I just need a small building for some staff like the head maid, the driver and anyone else I may need at short notice. The rooms do not need to be that big," said Bassem.

"I see." Blake nodded. "What do you think of the design of the house?" She wanted to know if he liked her style or not. It was important to keep him happy. Michaela had emphasized it to her.

"It's not bad," he said. Blake raised her eyebrows. She wanted more than that. "I must say your work is better than that of your peers. Though it needs some adjustments," he added. Blake smiled.

"I am pleased that you like my work," she said even though he had not said that he liked it. He had said that it was not bad. She could only assume that he liked it because he didn't ask for a new architect nor did he tell her to redo the entire house.

"I never said that I liked it," said Bassem.

"You never said that you did not like it either."

Bassem raised his eyebrows. "I have a short business trip to go on. So will I come in on Monday to see the revisions," said Bassem. He rose to his feet. Blake also rose to her feet.

"Yes, sheikh," she replied. "I hope you have a safe trip."

Bassem nodded and then walked out of her office. Blake was left standing in her office feeling rather confused. She had witnessed two different sides of Bassem. He was different outside the office. He was more friendly and fun. In the office, he was strict and serious. She was just grateful that he had not disliked her work and dismissed her from the project.

Blake sat down at her desk. She grabbed a pencil and a blank piece of paper. She often did a quick sketch of the design before she used the BIM software. Once again she had a short amount of time to complete her design. Bassem was not giving her a lot of time. He wanted and expected her to work quickly and perfectly.

When it was lunchtime, CJ barged into Blake's office with brown paper bags in her hand. "You should knock," Blake said to her.

"I have food," she replied with a grin. She held up her brown paper bags.

"Come in." Blake put her pencil down. CJ quickly approached the desk and sat down on the chair opposite Blake.

"Did Bassem like your work?" CJ opened the brown paper bag and took the food out. She passed Blake her food and a pair of chopsticks.

"He said it was not bad." Blake inhaled the scent of her noodles. She was quite hungry.

"Not bad? That is the nicest thing he has ever said to anyone in this company." CJ laughed a little. "He hated everything that I designed for him." CJ started eating fried rice.

"He wanted a few things to be redone and had a few additions." Blake took a mouthful of her noodles and chewed.

"That is a good sign. I guess dancing with him last night was a good move."

"He acted as though last night never happened."

"What do you mean?" CJ and Blake swapped their food. They always bought different food and then shared it.

"He did not smile at me nor did he say anything about last night." Blake took a mouthful of CJ's fried rice.

"That's weird." CJ frowned.

"Tell me about it. I asked him if he had gotten home very late and he said no. But the way he answered me, he looked at me as though he was wondering why I was asking," said Blake.

"He is really a strange man. He was really nice last night, and the two of you spent so much time together," CJ replied.

"I guess I will just have to forget about last night and focus on my work."

CJ shook her head. "Rich men are always strange. They're either workaholics or playboys or have a sex dungeon in their homes," she said. Blake narrowed her gaze at CJ.

"Sex dungeons?" she questioned. CJ burst into laughter.

"It happens. Rich men always have weird sexual desires," she said. Blake shook her head.

"I am sure that has nothing to do with being rich. Even men working minimum wage jobs can have weird sexual desires."

CJ smiled. She looked at her watch. "I have to eat fast. I have a client coming in five minutes," she said. CJ and Blake swapped their food again.

"You better hurry," said Blake.

Chapter 5

The flight attendant greeted Bassem with a big smile on her face as he walked onto his private jet. He greeted her and then headed over to the seating area. He sat down in the beige leather seat. He buckled his seat belt and waited for takeoff. He was flying out to Mexico for a few days. He was meeting with a client to finalize a deal.

They took off moments later. Bassem started thinking about his meeting with Blake. He was pleasantly surprised at the design that she had showed him. She had designed a pretty decent house. He was impressed that she was able to design such a nice house within three days. He wondered why Michaela had not put Blake on the project in the first place.

Bassem's jet landed in Mexico about two and a half hours later. They landed at a private airstrip. There was a car already waiting for Bassem. The driver took him straight to his meeting. He was meeting with a Mexican mogul, Mathew Rodriguez. He was a very rich man that owned a lot of gas stations in Mexico.

When Bassem arrived at Mr. Rodriguez's company, the receptionist escorted him to the conference room. Bassem's business lawyers had already arrived. They had flown in from Austin a little bit earlier than

Bassem. They greeted the sheikh with bows when he walked into the room.

Moments later, Mr. Rodriguez and his lawyers walked into the conference room. Mr. Rodriguez shook Bassem's hand. "It is good to see you again, sheikh," he said to him.

"I trust that you have been well since we last met," Bassem said.

"I have." Mr. Rodriguez smiled.

They all sat down at the conference table. Bassem and Mr. Rodriguez had been communicating for months about doing business together. They were finally going to sign the contracts and make it official. Bassem's company was to supply Mr. Rodriguez's company with fuel to sell at their gas stations. Bassem was to get a large percentage of the profits made from the sales. Mr. Rodriguez was to also receive a percentage.

Bassem had wanted to extend his business beyond the United States. So when he heard about Mr. Rodriguez looking for a new oil supplier, he took the chance. His father had sent him to improve business in Austin and that was exactly what he was going to do.

"We will start with a three-year contract. The three years will be a trial for us both. If after three years we are not on the same business terms, then we part ways. If we are happy, then we sign a contract for a longer term," said Bassem.

"I completely agree," said Mr. Rodriguez.

"Excellent." Bassem nodded.

"We are requesting 30% of your profits."

Bassem barely reacted. "We are offering 20%," he said. Mr. Rodriguez raised his eyebrows.

"20% is a bit low."

"We sell high-quality oil. It has been quite popular in the United States. I am sure that we will have high profits here too. 20% will be a lot of money."

Bassem's secretary gave Mr. Rodriguez a report on their profits. Mr. Rodriguez looked surprised as he studied the document.

"We expect to see an increase in our profits," said Bassem.

"Okay. How about 25%?" said Mr. Rodriguez.

"20%."

"24%?"

"21%."

Mr. Rodriguez laughed. "Okay, I will agree to 21%," he said. "You are a tough negotiator," he added. Bassem smiled.

"I am glad we can agree on a percentage," he said. The two men laughed.

"I was warned that you are stricter than your father."

"By whom?"

"My father," said Mr. Rodriguez. Bassem crossed his eyebrows. "My father once had business with your father."

"I did not know that," Bassem replied.

"Nothing was ever signed. They had a short-term business agreement many years ago."

"I see."

"When I spoke to my father about going into business with you, he advised that it was a good idea. He also told me that he had heard about you being very strict in business," said Mr. Rodriguez.

"Is that the reputation I have acquired?" Bassem laughed. Mr. Rodriguez laughed and nodded. Now that they had agreed on their business arrangement, Bassem and Mr. Rodriguez agreed to have contracts finalized and then sign them the next day.

***

Blake yawned as she stretched. She had been working on her designs for the sheikh for hours. She just needed to take a break. She slipped on her oversized grey hoodie and then headed out of her apartment. She decided to go and get some ice cream. The walk to the shop would help her clear her mind.

As she was walking to the shop, a car's horn beeped at Blake. She turned her head and saw a Rolls-Royce Phantom pulling up. The window rolled down. She stopped walking and looked to see who it was. Bassem poked his head out of the window. Blake gasped. Of all times to run into Bassem; she was wearing grey leggings, a hoodie and Puma slides.

"We meet again," he said to her.

"Yes, well we met on Thursday and we are meeting again on Monday," she replied. He smiled at her.

"Do you live around here?"

"Yes I do, just over there." Blake pointed at the apartment complex.

"Where are you going?"

"To buy some ice cream."

"Hop in, I'll take you."

Blake raised her eyebrows. Hop in? That did not sound like something Bassem would say, she thought to herself. She looked at him. He was being friendly to her once again.

"It's okay, sheikh. I can go by myself," she said.

"Come on." He opened the door for her. Blake got into the car and sat opposite him. The interior of the car was impressive. The beige leather seats were comfortable. They were finished with a wooden armrest. Bassem ordered his driver to take them to a nearby ice cream parlor.

Bassem was wearing a white shirt and navy blue trousers. Blake noticed his hair was parted from the right side instead of the left. Bassem probably had different personalities. He was different outside the office to how he was inside the office.

"How have you been spending your weekend?" he asked her.

"I was working on your house," she said. Bassem raised his eyebrows.

"Why do that over the weekend?"

"Huh? Well you told me to have it done by Monday. So, I definitely have to work during the weekend."

Bassem smiled. "Well I appreciate your hard work," he said to her.

"What brings you to this side of town?" she asked him.

"I was just meeting with a friend," he replied.

"Ah. How was your trip?"

"It went well."

They pulled up at an ice cream parlor moments later. Blake and Bassem got out of the car and walked towards the entrance of the shop. Bassem opened the door for Blake.

"Thank you," she said before she walked into the shop. They walked up to the counter and looked at the menu.

"What do you feel like having?" Bassem asked her.

"I'll have number 23." She pointed at the menu.

"That has a lot of cookies and candies in it."

"Yes." Blake grinned. She had a sweet tooth.

"I'll have mine plain with cherry sauce."

"That is so plain."

Bassem laughed a little. He ordered for both and then paid. They took their ice creams and went to sit down at a table. Blake tasted her ice cream. "This tastes so good," she said. Bassem frowned at her.

"All of that will make your stomach hurt," he said.

"No, it will not." Blake ate another spoonful. "Would you like to taste it?"

"There is no way I am eating that." Blake and Bassem burst into laughter.

They engaged in conversation as they ate their ice cream. Bassem teased Blake about her ice cream. He was quite cheeky and funny. It still shocked her how his personality could change that much.

After they were finished eating, she decided to walk home because she hadn't gotten any exercise yet. "See you soon," he said to her.

"See you Monday." Blake smiled and waved him.

Chapter 6

Bassem stepped out of the shower and wrapped the towel around his waist. He headed back into his room to get dressed. He had a small house in Austin that he had purchased. He was going to live there until his new house was built and ready for moving into.

As he was getting dressed, his cell phone rang. He picked it up from the nightstand and answered it.

"Hello," he answered.

"Bassem, it's your mother," a voice sounded from the receiver.

"I know your voice, Mother." Bassem put the phone on speaker and put it down on the nightstand.

"Well, it has been long since you called me. I wouldn't be surprised if you didn't recognize my voice."

Bassem rolled his eyes. His mother was always dramatic. "I have been tied up with work," he replied.

"Even so, you should always make sure to call me at least once a day."

"Once a day?" Bassem did not have that much time on his hands. He slipped into a pair of grey trousers.

"Yes. Anyway, how have you been?"

"I've been well."

"Do you have a lover?"

"This is not a conversation I am willing to have with you."

His mother burst into laughter. "You are so different to your brother. He has a new woman every other day," she said.

"That's his business," he said. His mother sighed.

"I am so thankful that you have never had a scandal."

"My brother has only had two scandals," Bassem said.

"Two is too many!" his mother cried out. "I need the two of you to settle down this year," she added.

"This year is a bit too soon."

"No, it is not. You are already thirty years old. You don't want to end up getting married at forty."

"Forty sounds like a nice age to wed," Bassem teased his mother.

"Do not say things like that," she snapped. Bassem laughed. He started buttoning up his pink shirt.

"I have to go," he said to his mother. "I have to meet with the architect in half an hour."

"Okay. Make sure you call me more often," she replied. Bassem hung up the phone. He brushed his hair and then slipped into his loafers. He sprayed on a little bit of cologne before he left his house.

***

Bassem arrived at Collette Architects almost twenty minutes later. The perky receptionist escorted him to Blake's office.

"Good morning, sheikh," Blake greeted him as he walked into her office. She was wearing a cream skirt that complemented her curves and a sky-blue striped shirt. She had her hair tied up into a tight ponytail.

"Good morning, Miss Gordon," Bassem replied.

"Please have a seat."

"Sure." Bassem sat down on the chair at her desk. Her office was clean and tidy as always. He appreciated her tidiness. He disliked women that were not tidy.

"Shall I get you anything to drink?" she asked him.

"No, thank you."

"How about ice cream?" Blake smiled brightly.

"I don't like ice cream," he replied. Blake's eyes widened.

"Really?"

"Why do you look so surprised?"

"I thought you liked ice cream," she mumbled as she sat down in her chair. She stared at him with such a confused facial expression. It was as if she was trying to figure something out.

"Why would you think that?" he asked her.

"No reason." Blake shrugged her shoulders. "Here are the designs." She handed him the folder.

He flipped though the designs and carefully looked at the corrections she had done. He was impressed with her quality of work. She was quite creative and she met her deadlines. He looked up from the sketches and found Blake's large green eyes fixed on him.

"Is there something you wish to say to me?" Bassem asked Blake.

"I… um…" Blake cleared her throat. "No there isn't."

"Are you sure?"

"Yes."

She still looked very confused. Bassem wondered what was going on in her head. There was clearly something on her mind.

"Anyway, I will go ahead with these designs," he said. Blake raised her eyebrows.

"Really? You like them?" she asked.

"They're not bad."

Blake smiled. "I am glad you like them," she said.

"I appreciate you finishing the sketches on time," he said to her.

"It was not easy," she admitted.

"We will have to break ground this week. I am looking for this house to be done as soon as possible," he said.

"It is such a big house. It will take a while to complete."

"I am looking to move in within six months."

"That means you need a lot of builders, and they will need to work long hours," Blake said.

"That will be your job."

"Sheikh?"

"You will be supervising the project from start to end. You will be in charge of hiring all the construction workers, plumbers, electricians and any other engineers you may need."

"You wish to have me in charge?" she asked.

"It is your project," Bassem replied.

"I am used to supervising all projects but not being so hands-on."

"You don't have the confidence to get the job done?"

"No, I can do it."

"Good." Bassem rose to his feet. "Come to my office on Wednesday. We will finalize everything and then we will go to the site," he said to her. Blake sprang to her feet.

"Yes sir," she replied.

"Don't make me regret hiring you."

"Yes sir."

"Why do you keep looking at me in such a strange way?"

"Am I?" Blake gasped.

"Is there something on your mind?"

"Yes there is."

"Is it something you wish to share with me?"

Blake smiled and shook her head. "It's not a big deal, apparently," she said. Bassem crossed his eyebrows. She was behaving rather strangely.

"Okay." He turned and left her office. The perky receptionist sprang up to her feet as Bassem walked into the reception area.

"Are you leaving already?" she asked Bassem.

"Yes," he replied. She bowed her head to him.

"Have a good day, sheikh," she said.

"Mmm, thanks." Bassem raised an eyebrow. The receptionist was always overly cheerful. It was too much for him.

Chapter 7

Blake sat on her desk and just shook her head. Bassem was so confusing. She couldn't keep up with his personality changes. On Saturday, they were eating ice cream and laughing together. Now he was telling her that he did not like ice cream. Blake wanted to kick herself for not directly asking him about it. She hadn't because she was caught off guard, and if he was not mentioning it then she wasn't going to.

"Blake!" CJ yelled out as she walked into Blake's office.

"Don't you have work to do?" Blake asked her.

"I just finished meeting with a client. So, I decided to come and see you before I returned to my office." CJ quickly approached Blake.

"I see."

"How did it go with the sheikh?"

"Well, he liked my final designs and said he wants me to manage the entire process."

"Well that is expected."

"No, he wants me fully involved. I have to hire the builders and all that stuff."

CJ raised her eyebrows. "I guess he trusts you since the two of you have been hanging out together outside the office," she said and then grinned mischievously.

"It's definitely not that. He still pretends as though it never happened," said Blake.

"He did it again?"

"I offered him ice cream as a joke and he said that he did not like ice cream."

CJ burst into laughter. "He is a very strange man," she said.

"Tell me about it."

"Well why didn't you bring it up?"

"I don't know." Blake shrugged her shoulders. "I guess I was waiting for him to bring it up," she said.

"You should have said something about it."

"Like what? And what if he denied it?"

"Then the next time you meet up, confront him about it."

"Or avoid him completely," said Blake. CJ laughed.

"Just ask him about it the next time you see him," said CJ. Blake sighed.

"I have to see him on Wednesday." Blake frowned as she tried to imagine herself talking to Bassem about it. She didn't even know what she would say.

"I can't believe he liked your work so quickly." CJ sighed. "But then again you are extremely talented. So, if he didn't like your work, then he would be an idiot," she added.

"Thank you." Blake grinned.

Michaela suddenly barged into Blake's office.

"Blake, you've done it!" she cried out.

"Why don't people knock?" Blake mumbled quietly.

"What has she done?" CJ asked.

"I just received a call from the sheikh's secretary. The sheikh likes your work and he is going to go ahead and build the house as per your designs," Michaela explained. Blake smiled.

"Yes, he did say that he wanted to meet me on Wednesday. He wants to start building as soon as possible," she said. Michaela smiled and clapped her hands together.

"This is great news," said Michaela. "I knew I could count on you."

"Thank you."

"If you need anything, don't hesitate to come to me."

Blake and CJ looked at each other. Michaela was never that friendly. She was always serious and strict. Blake could see that her boss was excited about the money they could make from working for the sheikh.

***

On Wednesday morning, Blake made sure that she arrived at the sheikh's office early. She had to do everything correctly. She could not afford to make a single mistake. The sheikh had had so many architects already. It showed her that he was a no-nonsense man. He would fire anyone in a heartbeat.

Blake straightened her navy blue dress before she headed into the large building. She walked into the lobby of the office. She walked up to the reception.

"Good morning. My name is Blake Gordon. I am here to see Sheikh Sedarous," Blake said to the receptionist.

"Good morning, Miss Gordon. Do you have an appointment?" the receptionist replied.

"Yes, I do."

"Okay, one moment." The receptionist picked up the phone and called someone. "Hello, I have Miss Gordon at reception. Okay." She put the phone down and looked at Blake. "Please take the elevator to the tenth floor. The sheikh's secretary will meet you there and take you to the sheikh's office," she said to Blake.

"Okay, thank you," Blake replied. She walked over to the elevator and pressed the button.

When Blake reached the tenth floor, a tall, neatly dressed woman greeted her. "Hello, my name is Amina. I am the sheikh's secretary," she said.

"Hello Amina," Blake greeted her.

"The sheikh is expecting you. Please follow me this way."

"Sure."

Blake followed Amina down the wide, clean hallways. Amina knocked on the door before she opened it for Blake. Blake thanked Amina and then walked in.

"Oh, my God!" Blake spat out as she walked in. There were two Bassems. One wore black trousers and a navy blue shirt. The other was wearing black trousers and a maroon shirt. They both had the same hairstyle and beard. The two men were leaning against the desk talking.

"There's two of you." Blake crossed her eyebrows and shifted her gaze from one to the other. She was trying to figure out which one was Bassem.

"Hello Miss Gordon," said the one in the navy blue shirt.

"We meet again," the one in the maroon shirt said with a smile. Blake looked at the one in the navy blue shirt.

"You must be Bassem," she said. She looked at the one in the maroon shirt. "And you are?"

"Basil," he said with a smile.

"This is crazy." Blake ran her hand through her hair.

"Yes, I have a brother," said Bassem.

"This explains a lot."

"What?"

Blake looked at Basil. "Why didn't you tell me sooner that you weren't Bassem?" she asked him. He flashed a mischievous grin.

"It was funny," he admitted. Blake's jaw hung open.

"What is going on?" Bassem asked.

"It was all so weird and frustrating," said Blake.

"I am sorry," said Basil.

"Sorry for what?" Bassem asked.

"I met your brother at a nightclub thinking that it was you. You came to my office the next day acting differently. I was wondering why you were pretending not to remember us hanging out," she explained. Bassem raised his eyebrows.

"Hanging out?" he asked.

"Oh no!" Blake put her hands out to protest. "Nothing sexual," she added. Basil started laughing.

"My brother and I are so different. You must have had a hard time," he said.

"Yes, I did," said Blake. Bassem smiled for the first time since Blake had met him.

"My brother is always up to no good. I apologize for the misunderstanding," he said.

"It's okay," Blake mumbled.

"Miss Gordon is an architect," Bassem explained to Basil.

"I see," said Basil. He extended his hand out to Blake. "Well, it is nice to officially meet you, Miss Gordon."

"Please call me Blake." Blake shook his hand.

"Okay, Blake." Basil smiled. "I will leave the two of you alone. I will make it up to you sometime."

"Yes, you really need to do that because that was a horrible prank. It's a good thing I did not confront the sheikh about ignoring me and then make a fool out of myself," she said. Basil laughed.

"That would have been so funny." He winked at Blake before he headed out of Bassem's office.

"Would you like to have a seat?" Bassem asked Blake.

"Yes please," she replied. She sat down on the sofa in his office. Bassem sat down opposite her.

"How many times did you meet my brother?" Bassem asked.

"We met only twice. The first time was at a club and the second time it was outside my apartment and we went for ice cream," Blake replied.

"Ah, that was why you offered me ice cream."

"Yeah." Blake laughed. She felt weird discovering that Bassem had a twin. However, she was glad that that situation had been resolved. It was even better that she had walked in on the two of them together because she had gone to see him with the intention of asking him about the club and the ice cream. If she didn't ask, it was going to be weird for her to continue working with him.

"You should have told me about it," Bassem said to her.

"I didn't know what to say and it was embarrassing," she replied.

"Why was it embarrassing?"

"I was thinking that you were pretending that nothing ever happened. So me bringing it up was awkward and embarrassing."

Bassem started laughing at her. Blake raised her eyebrows. He had smiled and laughed in one day. It was shocking. The previous times she had met with him, he had been so serious. It was as if he wasn't capable of smiling.

Chapter 8

There was a knock on the door. "Yes?" Bassem called out. Amina swung the door open and walked in holding a tray with two cups and a glass coffeepot on it. She approached the sheikh and Blake with a smile on her face.

"I brought some coffee," she announced as she placed the tray down on the table. The sheikh nodded in response. She poured the coffee into the cups before she left the office. The sheikh gestured for Blake to have her coffee.

"Thank you," she said as she reached out for one of the white mugs.

"It's Lebanese coffee," he said to her.

"Really?" Blake inhaled the scent of the coffee before she took a sip. "It tastes good." She had never tried Lebanese coffee before.

"Yes, the coffee has a rich and strong flavor," Bassem added.

"You're a coffee person?"

"I don't understand what that means."

Blake smiled. "People often like either tea or coffee. I prefer coffee; therefore I am a coffee person," she said.

"I like both equally," said Bassem.

"I failed to like tea."

"You just haven't tasted the right one."

"So you like tea but dislike ice cream," she said cheekily before she took a sip of her coffee. He had told her that he didn't like ice cream when she had offered it to him at the office. It was still odd to her that it was his twin brother that she had spent time with.

"You find that peculiar?" he asked her.

Blake nodded. "I've never heard of anyone disliking ice cream. It's like hating Christmas," she said.

Bassem shrugged his shoulders unapologetically. "I will need for you to go and inspect the site where I want to build my house," he changed the subject. The informal conversation had lasted for a very short period. He was such a serious man and rarely smiled.

"Yes sir," Blake replied.

"When we are done here, my driver will take you there."

"I brought my car with me, I can drive there myself."

"Very well," Bassem replied. "I have already had the site surveyed for environmental hazards and there are none."

"That makes my job easier." Blake smiled. It was part of her job to make sure that the building site was safe to build on.

"In our next meeting, I will need you to bring me estimated budgets," Bassem said to Blake before he took a sip of his coffee. Blake nodded. "I will need you to look into contractors, engineers, plumbers and electricians."

"You don't have to worry about all of that. I will get you all the information you need. Your house is in safe hands." She flashed a smile.

"I did not think your hands were dangerous," he replied.

"I meant that I will do my job very well."

"I hope so because I do not give second chances." Bassem wore such a serious facial expression. His intense gaze sent chills down Blake's spine. He made her nervous.

"I see," she replied.

"Do you have any questions for me?"

"No, I do not."

"Very well then, my secretary will give you the address on your way out."

Blake and Bassem both rose to their feet. Blake bid the sheikh farewell before she headed for the door. She stopped by his secretary's desk which was located outside his office. Amina gave her the address to the site where Bassem wanted to build his house.

When Blake was in her car, she keyed the address into the navigator. She stuck the key into the ignition and pulled away from the parking lot. The site was about a fifteen-minute drive from the sheikh's office. Bassem had bought his land in an affluent part of Austin.

***

The next morning it was Blake's turn to barge into CJ's office. She made sure she didn't have a client before she walked in. "Morning, Cora," she said with a cheerful smile. CJ frowned at her.

"Only Michaela and my mom seem to enjoy calling me Cora," she replied as she leaned back into her chair. Blake grinned. She only called her by her first name when she wanted to annoy her. CJ didn't like her first name because she was named after her aunt whom she didn't get along with.

"I have figured out why the sheikh was ignoring the time we spent together." Blake plonked herself in the chair at CJ's desk. CJ's eyes widened.

"You confronted him about it! What did he say?"

"I didn't have to confront him."

"Then what?" CJ frowned.

"I walked into his office and saw him there with his brother. CJ, he has an identical twin brother!" Blake explained.

"What?" CJ spat out. "No way!"

"All this time his brother led me on."

CJ started laughing. "Were they playing a trick on you?" she asked. Blake shook her head.

"Bassem didn't know about it. Basil; that's the brother's name, he was laughing about it. Come to think of it, he didn't offer an explanation. He just said that it was funny," said Blake.

CJ crossed her arms over her chest. "He seems to be playful and cheeky. That is the opposite of Bassem. What did Bassem even say about it?" she replied.

"He laughed and said his brother was up to no good again."

"He wasn't angry about it?"

"No, he wasn't. It was my first time seeing him laugh." Blake sighed. "He's just so serious."

CJ raised her eyebrows. "So are you," she said.

"Excuse me?"

"You can be quite serious."

"Can be but not always."

CJ narrowed her gaze at her. "You know how uptight you are. You and Bassem actually suit. You're similar." CJ started stroking her chin as if she was deeply thinking about it. Blake raised an eyebrow.

"How are we similar?" Blake asked.

"You're both perfectionists."

"That's only one thing we have in common. It doesn't mean that we are similar."

"You're both serious and uptight."

Blake rolled her eyes. "Okay, Cora." She rose to her feet. She turned and headed towards the exit. She slowly headed back to her office. She knew that she and Bassem didn't suit. CJ was just being mischievous as always. However, CJ was right about her being uptight. She wasn't as free-spirited as CJ was. She didn't know to just let go and have some fun. She needed CJ for that. CJ was always prompting her to relax and have more fun. She was the life of the party not Blake.

Blake walked into her office and shut the door behind her. She needed to do the expense report for the sheikh. He wanted her to give him an estimated budget for the entire project. To do that, she had to compile a list of materials needed to build the entire house and calculate how much they would cost. She also needed to find builders and engineers, and calculate how much their services were going to cost.

Chapter 9

Bassem was sitting in the living room reading a newspaper when his brother walked in uninvited. Bassem looked up from the newspaper. "Can I help you with something?" he asked.

"Am I not allowed to visit my only brother?" Basil asked as he planted himself on the sofa opposite his brother. Bassem folded the newspaper and put it down on the coffee table.

"Have you gotten yourself into trouble again?"

"I don't get into trouble." Basil flashed a cheeky grin.

"For now."

"No more. I have turned a new leaf."

"Our mother would be glad to hear of it," said Bassem. "She called me the other day."

"She asked of me?" Basil asked. Bassem shook his head.

"She mentioned that she wanted us to settle down."

"Wives?" Basil burst into laughter. "I am not the marrying type. I'll leave that to you."

Bassem raised an eyebrow. "To me?" he asked.

"You are more responsible, mature and smart. You'd make a good husband."

"And you don't possess those qualities?"

"No I don't. That's why you're the crown prince and not me."

"Well, I am older than you. So naturally I would be the crown prince."

"You're older by four minutes and eighteen seconds," Basil clarified. Bassem laughed a little.

"I am still older," he replied.

"Father knows that you would make a better king than I would. He made a wise decision."

"He did?"

"I don't like being tied down to a situation. So, since you are the crown prince, you have to get married anyway. You can't be a king without a queen or an heir."

Bassem groaned. His brother was very right. Marriage was inevitable for him. He had to get married no matter what. He just hoped that his future wife was a quiet and well-mannered one.

One of Bassem's maids walked into the room and bowed her head to the princes. "Dinner is ready," she announced.

"Good," Basil said as he sprang to his feet. "I was starving."

The two brothers headed over to the dining room. They sat down at the table and waited for the maids to serve them.

"How's that architect of yours?" Basil asked Bassem.

"Miss Gordon? Why are you bringing her up?" Bassem replied.

"She's such an interesting woman."

"Is that why you pretended to be me?"

"I was in the club when she and her friend approached me. They both thought that I was you."

"You should have corrected her."

"And spoil the fun?" Basil started laughing. "I'm surprised that she didn't say anything to you."

"So am I." Bassem picked up a fork and started eating.

"I feel bad for her. I must make it up to her," Basil replied. He picked up his glass and took a sip of his drink.

"What are your intentions?"

Basil put his hands up. "Oh no, it's not like that at all," he said. Bassem raised an eyebrow.

"You're not attracted to her?" he asked.

"No, I'm not. She is an attractive woman but she seems a little bit too serious for me."

Bassem shook his head. "You like them wild and freaky," he said.

"Exactly." Basil grinned.

"Just make sure you don't end up in the tabloids again," Bassem warned.

"I won't." Basil cut a piece of his lamb and ate it. "What are you going to do with this house when you're finished building your new home?" he asked.

"I'll sell it."

"You should have just stayed in a hotel."

"I don't like hotels."

"If it weren't for the fact that we are identical, I'd think that we weren't brothers at all," said Basil. Bassem looked at his brother.

"Please elaborate," he said.

"We are so different."

"Siblings don't always have to have a lot in common all the time."

"You're also strange. Who doesn't like hotels?" Basil shook his head.

"Public places are always crawling with germs," Bassem replied.

"They have cleaners at hotels."

"There are too many people at hotels. You know how I like my privacy."

"I agree with that. There's a lack of privacy in hotels."

The two brothers enjoyed a light conversation as they ate their dinner. Basil contributed the most to the conversation. He was always the more vocal twin.

***

Blake was just sitting at her office desk working when a loud knock on the door disturbed her thoughts. She looked up from her laptop and called out, "Come in!"

The door swung open and in walked Bassem or Basil. Blake was not sure which one of the brothers it was. She rose to her feet and stared at the tall, muscular, handsome man as he walked towards her. She studied him for clues as to his identity.

"Basil," she said at last. He flashed a toothy grin.

"How could you tell?" he asked her.

"Your side parting is on the right side."

Basil laughed. "I'll make sure to part from the left side next time," he said. He leaned over the desk and pressed his lips against Blake's right cheek. She raised her eyebrows in response. She wasn't expecting him to kiss her nor was she used to him. It felt like it was Bassem kissing her and it made her feel nervous.

"Have a seat," she said to him. Basil lowered himself into the black tufted chair and made himself comfortable. He put a plastic bag on the table and started fishing out the contents. Blake stared at him wondering what he had.

"I brought lunch," he said to her.

"Lunch?"

Basil opened the containers and gave Blake a fork. "Pita bread, lamb, hummus and ice cream," he said.

"Sounds good." Blake took the fork from him, then took a small piece of the lamb and put it in her mouth. She savored the taste as she chewed. "Tastes good."

"Arabic food tastes good." Basil started eating also.

"So, what brings you to my office?"

"I came to apologize for impersonating my brother."

"Do you trick people often?"

"I am a twin." Basil shrugged his shoulders. "Of course, I would use that to have some fun."

Blake shook her head. "You don't know how awkward it was to face your brother after meeting you. I just couldn't understand why he was acting as though nothing happened. I was starting to get offended," she said. Basil burst into laughter.

"That's so funny," he said.

"It wasn't funny for me," Blake said, but then she laughed a little. Now that the misunderstanding had been resolved, she found the whole situation a little amusing.

"How is it working with my brother?"

"It's fine."

Basil raised his eyebrows. "I don't believe you," he said.

"Why not?"

"He's a perfectionist, a strict, short-tempered perfectionist. I can't imagine that it's easy working with him."

Blake smiled. "I like working with people that know what they want," she said.

"I see."

"How did you even know where I work?" Blake asked. She had never told him where she worked.

"My brother told me." Basil leaned back in his chair. "I don't see a ring on your finger."

"I'm only twenty-six; there is no rush to get married."

65

"Boyfriend?"

"No."

Basil finished his lamb and then moved on to the ice cream. "Why architecture?" he asked.

"Huh?"

"Why did you become an architect?"

"I always had an interest in buildings and I've always been good at drawing and designing things."

"That simple?"

"Yes." Blake laughed. "There's no specific reason as to why I chose this career. I guess I just knew from an early age that this is what I wanted, and I've never thought about anything else," she added.

"And you're enjoying your job?"

"Yes, I love it." Blake opened the small container with her ice cream that Basil had bought for her. She smiled when she saw so many sweet toppings on her ice cream.

"I knew you'd like it," Basil said to her. Blake laughed.

"Thank you."

Blake and Basil talked more about her job and about her life. He was very friendly and easy to talk to. Blake was glad that Basil had come to visit her because she had enjoyed a free meal and good company.

Chapter 10

Bassem walked into his living room and found Blake standing there studying the room. She was dressed in a thin-strapped grey dress that hugged her curves, and sandals. Bassem had things to discuss with her, so he had asked Amina to call Blake over to his home.

"Do you like what you see?" he asked Blake. She turned to face him.

"I think this room is a bit too narrow. I would rather it was a bit wider, but I do like the arched doorway," she replied. Bassem smiled.

"Spoken like a true architect."

"I can't help but analyze buildings wherever I go."

"Good, I need someone that is really invested in their job." He gestured for Blake to sit.

"Thank you," she said as she sat down on the sofa. A maid walked into the room with a glass of cold orange juice for Blake.

"Shall I get you anything?" she asked the sheikh.

"No," he replied. The maid bowed her head and quickly left the room. The sheikh turned his attention to Blake. "Do you mind me asking to see you during the weekend?" he asked her.

"I was a bit surprised. I'd have assumed that you would be chilling and relaxing on weekends."

"I usually work during weekends."

"Oh."

"During the duration of this project, I need you to be fully accessible to me," he said.

"I see," Blake replied. "I am okay with that, as long as it is within reason."

"Please elaborate."

"I usually take my work home as well. However, if you call for me after 8 p.m. or on a Sunday, I won't be available."

Bassem was surprised at how assertive she was. Whenever he demanded something, no matter how unreasonable it was, people always gave into him. He was pleasantly surprised to see Blake setting boundaries.

"Very well," he replied. "Did I disrupt your plans today?"

"No, you didn't," Blake replied.

"You're dressed up."

"Not really." Blake smiled. "My friend and I were just at the park enjoying the sun with some ice cream."

"It sounds like you had plans."

"I work with her and we live in the same neighborhood. We didn't have special plans."

"I see." The sheikh cleared his throat. "I called you over to talk about the house because I'm leaving town tomorrow. So, I will not be available for a week or so."

"That is fine." Blake fished her tablet out of her bag. She swiped the screen and then passed the tablet to him. "Since I am here now, I might as well show you the budget list."

Bassem took the tablet and read through the list. "You've already found contractors?" he asked her.

"I contacted a company that I've worked with on previous projects. I prefer to do business with people I know and can trust. Is that okay with you?"

"It's fine with me, as long they do their jobs correctly."

"We can start building next week."

Before Bassem could reply, a loud laugh sounded from the hallway. He already knew who it was. It was Basil. He walked into the room.

"What are you doing to my maids?" Bassem asked Basil.

"What? I didn't do anything," he replied.

"I heard that flirtatious laugh."

Basil shrugged his shoulders and looked at Blake. "Blake is here," he said as he approached her. He lowered his torso and kissed her on both cheeks.

"How are you?" she asked him.

"I'm fine." He planted himself on the sofa next to her. "Is my brother making you work on a Saturday?"

"Why are you here?" Bassem asked Basil.

"I came to spend time with my older brother." He grinned at Bassem.

"You're the younger twin?" Blake asked Basil.

"By four minutes and eighteen seconds."

Blake laughed in response. "I see," she said. Bassem crossed his eyebrows. Blake and Basil seemed to be close. It didn't surprise him. His brother was always popular with women. However, Bassem found himself not wanting his brother to get close to Blake. He didn't understand why it bothered him, but he just didn't want his brother developing a romantic interest in her.

"We were actually discussing business before you walked in," Bassem said to his brother.

"Okay, you may continue. Don't mind me." He pulled his phone out of his pocket. Bassem shook his head. His brother was always relaxed and never doing anything productive with his time.

"Call me if there is anything that needs to be paid for while I'm not around," Bassem said to Blake.

"Call you directly?" Basil asked.

"Yes," Bassem answered his brother. He fished his phone out of his pocket and put it on the table. "Key your number in," he said to her.

"Yes sir." Blake took his phone and keyed her number into it. She called her phone and saved Bassem's number. Basil was sitting next to her and watching her the entire time. He looked rather amused.

"My brother never gives out his personal cell phone number to anyone that's not family or that he's not sleeping with," said Basil. Bassem rolled his eyes. Blake slowly raised her head and looked at Bassem.

"Really? Why not?" she asked him.

"He's antisocial."

"I am not antisocial," Bassem retorted. Blake smiled and put his phone on the table for him. Basil laughed as he rose to his feet.

"I have to go," he said. "There is someone I must meet."

"It was good to see you again," Blake said to him.

"Likewise." He rubbed her shoulder before he left the room.

Bassem sighed after his brother had left. Basil had interrupted their conversation. He couldn't even remember what else there was to discuss with Blake because he had lost his train of thought.

"You and Basil seem close," Blake said with a smile.

"We have no choice since we are brothers," he replied.

"I have no siblings."

"You don't?"

"No." Blake shook her head. "I just have CJ, my friend. I've known her for about fifteen years and so she's become a sister to me."

"I see." Bassem wasn't sure what else to say to her. He wasn't a very sociable person as his brother always pointed out. When someone opened up to him and started talking about their life, Bassem never knew what to say. He simply wasn't interested.

"You've met her before actually," said Blake.

"Have I?"

"Yes, Cora. She was assigned to your project before me," she replied. Bassem stared at Blake blankly. He had no idea who she was talking about. "Big curly brown hair, very talkative."

"Oh, her."

"Yes."

Bassem raised his eyebrows. "You have different personalities," he said.

"Yes." Blake laughed. "I guess that is why we complement each other."

Suddenly one of the security guards walked into the living room. He bowed his head to the sheikh before he spoke.

"Excuse me, sheikh, there is something I must tell you," he said to the sheikh. Bassem frowned.

"Do you have to tell me now?" he asked. He was in the middle of a conversation with Blake.

"Yes, I do. This concerns your brother."

"What about my brother?"

"He has been abducted."

"What? You are not making sense."

"I was monitoring the camera when a black van pulled up outside the gate, blocking your brother's path. A few men came out of the van and pulled the sheikh out of his car."

"Oh my God," Blake gasped. Bassem sprang up to his feet.

"Then what happened?" he asked.

"He was forced into the van. He tried to fight them off but he was outnumbered," the security guard replied. Bassem ran his hands through his hair, then put his hands on his hips. He couldn't believe what he was hearing.

"Where were the security guards when all of this was happening?" he asked.

"They were both shot," he replied. Blake placed her hands on her mouth and looked at Bassem.

Chapter 11

Bassem strode out of the room and down the hall as fast as he could. He rushed to the CCTV room so that he could see exactly what had happened to his brother. He heard the pitter-patter of Blake's footsteps behind him. Bassem walked into the security room. There was a security guard sitting at the desk.

"Sheikh," the security guard said as he rose to his feet.

"Show me what happened," Bassem demanded.

"Yes sheikh." The security guard zoomed in on the monitor showing the front gate and rewound the footage. "Here," he added and then left the footage to play for the sheikh.

The footage showed a black van driving up to the gate and blocking Basil's car. The windows rolled down and a man fired his AK47 at the two security guards that were guarding the gate. Then the van door slid open and four masked men rushed out. They opened Basil's car door and pulled him out of the car. Basil managed to throw a few punches but one masked man pointed a gun at his head. He was then forced into the van.

After seeing the van drive off, Bassem punched the table. "Who would dare to come to my house and abduct my brother?" he said. Blake was standing next to him completely frozen. She was not sure what to do or say. She was also worried for Basil.

"Excuse me, sheikh," a maid said as she walked into the room.

"What?" Bassem spat out.

"There is someone on the phone for you."

"Do I look like I am in the mood to be receiving calls?" he asked her. The maid swallowed nervously before she replied.

"The person says that it's about your brother." Her arms trembled as she handed the phone over to the sheikh. Bassem snatched the phone from her.

"Who is this?" he demanded.

"Sheikh Bassem," a hoarse voice replied, "if you wish to see your brother alive, you will have to pay 100 million dollars." Bassem crossed his eyebrows.

"I'm not giving you anything."

"I don't think you have a choice. I will give you 48 hours to decide what's more important to you, 100 million dollars or your brother's life. I believe the latter choice is of more importance."

"If you harm a single hair on my brother's head, I will decapitate you with my bare hands."

There was sinister laugh before the line went dead. Bassem groaned before he rammed his fist into the table. Blake gasped loudly.

"What did they say?" Blake asked.

"I have to give them one hundred million dollars if I wish to see Basil alive."

Blake's green eyes widened. She placed her hands on her heart. "Those jerks," she said.

"Call Badir," Bassem ordered the security guard.

"Yes, sheikh," he replied. He fished his phone out of his pocket and pressed a few buttons.

"Shouldn't we call the police?" Blake asked.

"No," Bassem replied. Blake stared at him in confusion. "I don't want the public to find out what happened to my brother. The last thing I need is for it to be all over the tabloids," he explained.

"Okay, but the police can help."

"They're too slow."

"Do you have another option then?"

"I have my own men that will do the job faster. You should go home."

Blake stared at Bassem in concern. "I don't mind sticking around," she said. Bassem shook his head.

"I'll have someone tail you home and make sure that you're okay."

"No, that's—" Before Blake finished speaking, Bassem cut her off.

"It's not up for discussion."

"Yes sheikh." Blake rubbed her arm before she headed out of the room.

"Badir is on his way," the security guard said to Bassem.

"Follow Blake home and make sure she gets home okay," Bassem ordered.

"Yes sheikh." The security guard scrambled out of the room. Bassem sighed and ran his hand through his hair.

Badir walked into the room minutes later. "I came as soon as I could," he said to Bassem. Badir was part of Al Huddah's secret service. Badir and his team were located in Austin to make sure that Bassem and Basil were safe.

"Someone has dared to come to my house and abduct my brother," said Bassem. Badir's eyebrows shot up into his forehead.

"They came here?"

"Yes." Bassem played the footage for Badir.

"That is strange," said Badir.

"What is?"

"That they would come to your house to abduct Prince Basil."

Bassem crossed his arms over his chest. "How did they know that my brother was here? Either they were stalking him or I was the target," he said. Badir nodded in agreement.

"I will get my men on this," he said.

"You must find my brother as soon as possible. The perpetrators called a few minutes ago and asked for 100 million dollars. They've given me 48 hours to decide."

Badir raised his eyebrows. "I will make sure that I find the prince within 48 hours," he said.

"Yes, because I'm not willing to give them anything. I want to find out who's behind all this mess and make him pay." Bassem was infuriated. He couldn't tolerate anyone trying to bring harm to those close to him.

***

It was Sunday afternoon and Blake was sitting in her living room watching TV when she started thinking about Bassem. She wondered how he was coping. She didn't have any siblings but she knew that she wouldn't be able to cope if something happened to CJ. She jumped up to her feet and grabbed her car keys. She scrambled out of the front door and left her apartment complex and headed over to Bassem's home.

One of the maids escorted Blake to Bassem's office when she arrived at his home. Blake took a deep breath and knocked on his door.

"Yes," Bassem replied. Blake turned the silver doorknob and pushed the door open. Bassem looked up from his desk and looked at Blake as she walked in. "What are you doing here?" he asked her.

"I came to check up on you," she replied as she approached his desk.

"I'm fine." Bassem sighed. Blake raised her eyebrows. She didn't believe him, but she didn't expect him to open up about his feelings so easily. Blake pulled out the chair from the desk and sat down opposite him.

"Have you received any more phone calls?" she asked. Bassem shook his head. Silence stretched between them. Blake wasn't sure what to say to him. She was sure that he was feeling worried and frustrated, and there was nothing she could say to him to make him feel better.

"I just hope he's okay," Bassem said at last.

"I'm sure he's fine," Blake replied. "If they harm him, then they lose leverage."

"Hmm." Bassem ran his hand through his hair. A knock sounded on the door and a maid walked into the room.

"Lunch is ready," she told the sheikh.

"I'm not hungry," Bassem retorted. Blake noticed the concerned look on the maid's face.

"Have you eaten anything today?" Blake asked Bassem.

"No."

"You should eat something, even if it's very small."

"I don't have an appetite."

"Not eating will not help your brother," Blake said gently. Bassem raised his eyebrows. "You need to eat and have strength. Let's stay positive."

Bassem sighed and then rose to his feet. He slowly headed for the door. Blake rose to her feet and followed Bassem. He headed down the hall and then through the living room into the dining room. He pulled a chair out from the table and took a seat. Blake sat down opposite him.

"Are you hungry?" he asked her.

"No, I'm fine," she replied.

"If I have to eat, then you have to as well." He turned his attention to one of the maids. "Bring another plate," he ordered her.

"Yes sheikh," she replied and scurried out of the room.

"I thought you said you were busy on Sundays," Bassem said to Blake.

"I'm not busy on Sundays. It's my lazy day."

"Lazy day?"

"I sleep in until late, eat and just watch TV all day."

"That explains how you are dressed today."

Blake's eyebrows shot up. "How am I dressed today?" she asked.

"You're always so meticulous about your clothes, and I've also noticed how clean your office is," he replied. Blake smiled. She was indeed careful about how she dressed at work. She always made sure to have a smart and neat appearance. Since it was Sunday, she was wearing a pair of grey leggings and an oversized grey T-shirt and white sneakers.

Blake laughed a little. "I like to be comfortable when I am at home," she replied. The maid walked into the room with a plate, a glass and cutlery for Blake.

"My mother is not going to take the news of my brother's abduction well," said Bassem. He cut a small piece of meat and ate it.

"You haven't told her?" Blake asked. Bassem shook his head. "How about your father?"

"I haven't told him either," Bassem replied. Blake sighed.

"It's not easy but I guess you have to."

Bassem took another bite of his meat and then just put his fork down and pushed his plate away. He picked up his glass and took a sip.

"You haven't eaten much," said Blake.

"I really don't have an appetite," he replied.

A tall man dressed in black walked into the room. He approached the sheikh and bowed to him. His hair was styled in a crew cut. He had a three-day-old beard that barely covered the deep scar on his cheek.

"Did you find anything?" Bassem asked him.

"The van was stolen from a plumbing company," the man replied. His husky voice gave Blake chills. She put her fork down and looked at Bassem.

"So?"

"We looked at the CCTV recording of when the van was stolen. We are looking for the man that stole the van."

"I need an answer later today otherwise heads will roll," Bassem said to him.

"Yes, your highness." The man bowed his head before he walked out of the room. Blake watched him leave and then turned her head to face Bassem.

"Who is he?" she asked him.

"He's my head of security, Badir," Bassem replied.

"Oh." That explained the thick Arabic accent.

"You could go home," Bassem said to Blake. She shook her head.

"I don't mind sticking around. Your brother is a friend of mine. I'm worried about him too," she replied. Bassem raised an eyebrow at her as he rose from his seat. He held his hand out to Blake and helped her up to her feet.

"Friends?" Bassem questioned as they headed to the living room.

"We got to know each other well when he was impersonating you."

"I see."

"He also brought lunch to my office and we talked."

"My brother is no good with women, stay away."

Blake smiled. "We are just friends," she said. Bassem slid in his hands in his pockets and just shrugged his shoulders.

They walked into the living room and sat down at the sofas. They talked as they waited for a phone call from the abductors or news from Bassem's men.

Chapter 12

"I don't class Pilates as exercise," said Bassem. Blake frowned at him.

"How can you say that with a serious face?" she asked him. Bassem shrugged his shoulders.

"To me, Pilates and yoga are not strenuous exercise. It's just stretching and posing."

"I can't believe my ears." She burst into laughter. "Pilates works for me, it keeps me in shape. It is a form of exercise," she added. Bassem didn't even know how they had ended up talking about exercising. They had been sitting in the living room talking for hours.

"You'll probably try to convince me that ballet is a sport," he said.

"Okay, I don't do ballet but apparently, it is a sport. I'm just not interested in it," she replied.

"I doubt that you play any sports?"

"And you do?"

"Of course."

"Don't say you play golf."

Bassem smiled. "I play golf as well as swimming and fencing," he said.

"Fencing?" Blake frowned.

"What is wrong with fencing?" Bassem asked.

"For us ordinary people, it's not a normal thing to do," Blake replied. Bassem was surprised at how interesting Blake was. She was so easy to talk to and had a great sense of humor. Her being around had helped him relax and just take his mind off his brother. Her presence was comforting.

"I appreciate you being here," he said to her. Blake looked at Bassem and took his hand into hers. Her hand was so soft and warm.

"This is not the kind of situation anyone should go through alone," she said. Bassem reached out and placed his hand on her cheek. He caressed her silky soft skin with his thumb. He slowly closed the gap between them. Just when their faces were inches away from each other, Badir walked into the room and bowed his head to the sheikh.

"We traced Prince Basil's phone. It pinged off a cell phone tower in Bear Creek," said Badir.

Bassem and Blake both rose up from the sofa quickly with similar expressions of shock on their faces. "You did?" Bassem asked Badir.

"Oh my God," Blake breathed.

"His cell phone pinged about an hour ago before it was switched off. I am going to send some men to search the area within a twenty-mile radius," the man said to the sheikh.

"That is a good idea, let's go."

"Sheikh, I don't think it's a good idea for you to come."

"I am coming along and that is not up for discussion." Bassem headed for the door. Blake rushed out after him. He stopped walking and turned to face her. "Where are you going?" he asked her.

"I'm coming with you of course," she replied.

"No, you are not."

"Yes, I am. We can stand here and waste time arguing about it or we can go out and look for Basil."

Bassem stared at Blake for a moment. She was so serious and didn't look like she was willing to back down. He sighed before he caved. "Fine," he said to her. He turned on his heel and headed down the hall.

There were a lot of men that served under the king's secret service getting ready to depart when Bassem walked outside.

"Your highness," they all said in chorus and bowed their heads to Bassem.

"I am coming with you all to search for my brother," he said.

"It is not safe for you, your highness," said one of the men. Bassem dismissed him with his hand.

"We have to find my brother as soon as possible, let's go." Bassem headed to one of the black SUVs with Blake behind him.

"Make sure no harm comes to his highness," Badir instructed the men.

"Yes sir," they all answered in chorus and then rushed off into the other SUVs. Badir rushed after Bassem and opened the backseat door for him.

"I will drive you and stay by your side," Badir said to the sheikh. "I must stay with you and make sure that you are safe."

"Suit yourself," Bassem replied. He turned to face Blake. "Must you come?" he asked her. Blake nodded.

"The both of you shouldn't be coming," Badir mumbled under his breath. Bassem shot him a glance from the corner of his eye. Badir cleared his throat and looked away. Blake got into the backseat of the car and buckled her seat belt. Bassem got in and sat down next to her.

Badir shut the door and then walked around the car to the driver's side. He got into the car and stuck the key into the ignition. And then they were off.

***

There were a couple of cars in front of their car and more cars behind them. Blake figured that they did that just in case something happened, and then the sheikh's car wouldn't be the first to get into an accident or something.

They had been driving for over two hours. She glanced over to Bassem to check how he was doing. He was sitting there emotionless. He wore such a stern facial expression. Blake couldn't guess what was going through his head. Bassem turned to face her.

"What?" he asked her.

"Nothing, just wondering what's going through your mind right now," she replied.

"I just hope that my brother is in one piece when I reach him."

Blake took Bassem's hand into hers. He looked at their hands and then at her. "He will be," she replied.

"How can you be so sure?"

"We have to have faith. Besides, if they harmed your brother, then they wouldn't be able to get their money. I am sure they want money."

Bassem didn't respond. He just stared at Blake for a moment without saying a word. Blake was always so confident around Bassem but now that he was so close to her and staring at her, she was feeling very shy and nervous. She looked down and then looked back up. Bassem was still looking at her. His intense gaze made her stomach knot up.

He leaned in closer to her until their faces were so close to each other. He caressed her cheek with his thumb as he searched her face. The car suddenly came to a halt.

"Ah, your highness?" Badir said awkwardly.

"What?" Bassem spat out.

Blake tucked a lock of hair behind her ear and looked away. She touched her face with the back of her hand. It felt warm; no doubt she had been blushing. She wondered if Bassem had been intending to kiss her. That was the second time they had been awkwardly staring at each other and then were interrupted before anything could transpire. Damn those people with bad timing, Blake thought to herself.

"This is the place where the prince's phone was turned off," Badir said to Bassem. Blake looked out of the window. They had stopped by the roadside. The road was in the middle of a forest. There was nothing but trees in sight. The other SUVs had also parked at the side of the road. The security guards got out of the cars.

"It's such a deserted area," said Blake.

"They probably ditched the phone here. I doubt that they were stupid enough to stick around in the same area where they ditched the phone," Bassem pointed out.

"Criminals usually get caught because of the stupidest mistake," said Badir. "We have to start searching this area and then expand our search."

"Okay." Bassem sighed. Badir got out of the car and went to talk to the other security guards. He seemed to be giving them orders. They all nodded and headed back to their SUVs.

Chapter 13

After driving around for what seemed like forever, they finally saw an old-looking cabin near a swamp. There was a van parked outside the cabin. Badir turned his head and looked at Bassem. They shared a look of suspicion and concern.

"Let's check it out," Bassem said to Badir.

"Yes sheikh." Badir nodded as he rolled the window down and stuck his hand out. He gestured for the SUV behind him to go first.

The SUV behind them overtook them and drove up to the cabin first. The security guards jumped out of the SUV with their guns drawn and scanned the area first before they broke into the cabin. Badir drove up closer to the cabin and parked a few yards from it. He turned to face Bassem. The sheikh gave him a nod. Badir bowed his head and then grabbed his gun and rushed out of the car.

A gunshot sounded, causing the birds to fly away and Blake to inhale sharply. Bassem turned and looked at her. "Are you okay?" he asked her.

"Just shocked, I've never heard a gunshot in person," she replied.

Suddenly some unfamiliar men walked out of the cabin with Bassem's men pointing their guns at them. Bassem unbuckled his seat belt.

"Where are you going?" Blake asked him.

"I need to know if they're my brother's abductors," he replied.

"That isn't wise."

"Stay here." Bassem held Blake's face in his hands and pressed his lips against hers. It was a quick kiss but Blake felt how soft and luscious his lips were. She raised her eyebrows and watched Bassem getting out of the car. He had kissed her so easily, as if it was a reflex, as if it was something they did all the time.

Blake was full of mixed emotions. She was startled because of the gunshots. She was worried for Basil's safety. She wondered if he was in that cabin. She hoped that he was there and unharmed. She was confused by Bassem's kiss. It was their first kiss and it looked as though he had done it instinctively. He hadn't thought about it, he had just done it.

She watched as Bassem approached the chaos. She saw him talking to the unfamiliar men. She wondered what he was saying to them. She could only assume that he was asking about his brother. There was one man that was doing most of the talking. Suddenly Bassem threw his fist into the man's jaw causing him to stumble backwards.

Blake gasped at Bassem's unquestionable strength. He had punched the other man without much effort at all but it had caused the other man to stumble. She wondered what he had said to Bassem that had angered him. As much as she wanted to get out of the car, she had to stay inside just like Bassem had asked her to do.

Suddenly one of Bassem's men walked out of the cabin with Basil. He rubbed his wrists as he walked out. His shirt was unbuttoned halfway down. Blake gasped as she placed her hands on her heart. She was so glad to see that he was okay. He had been gone for a day, but it felt as though he had been gone for ages. She watched Bassem and Basil look at each other and then exchange nods.

A few words were exchanged between Bassem and Badir. Badir bowed his head. Bassem and Basil headed towards the SUV Blake was in. She opened the door and rushed out of the car. "Basil!" she cried out with her arms wide open. He looked at Bassem with a questioning gaze. Bassem shrugged his shoulders and shook his head.

Blake wrapped her arms around Basil. "I'm so glad you're okay," she said to him. Basil pulled out of her embrace and held her shoulders.

"What are you doing here? This place isn't safe for you," he said.

"I tried to tell her," said Bassem.

"It wasn't safe for you either," Blake retorted. She turned her attention back to Basil. "We were both worried about you. We couldn't just sit at home and wait to hear back from Badir," she said to him. Basil smiled at her and rubbed her shoulders.

"I'm fine, thanks for coming along," he said. He leaned in closer to her and kissed her on the cheek. Bassem slightly crossed his eyebrows.

"Let's go," he said to them, interrupting their moment. Basil and Blake both turned their heads to look at him. "There's no reason to linger around," he added. He looked away and walked around the car to the driver's side.

"You're driving?" Blake asked.

"Yes," Bassem replied. Blake never expected the sheikh to drive himself. She turned on her heel and just as she was about to get into the backseat of the car, Bassem stopped her. "Sit in the front," he ordered.

"Um, okay." Blake headed for the passenger's seat and sat next to Bassem. Basil climbed into the backseat of the car.

"I'll just sit back here by myself," he said sulkily. Bassem looked in the rearview mirror.

"You'll survive," he said. The car key was still in the ignition. He turned it and the engine purred in response.

"How come you're driving?" Blake asked. She looked outside the window as they pulled away from the cabin. "And what is going to happen to those men?" she asked.

"Badir will deal with it."

"How?" Blake whipped her head in Bassem's direction.

"What are you thinking about right now?" Basil burst into laughter.

"Well, they're in the middle of a deserted forest by a swamp. With guns," Blake replied. Basil laughed even harder.

"Yes, and so?" Bassem replied. Blake raised an eyebrow.

"Oh my God," she whispered.

"Don't worry, Badir is a professional," said Basil. Blake whipped her head in his direction. She stared at him with her eyebrows raised.

"Are you serious right now?"

"Do you think anyone can just threaten a prince of Al Huddah and get away with it?"

"Exactly," said Bassem. Blake stared at Basil with a face full of concern. Basil burst into laughter.

"Relax, no one is going to die," he said to her.

"Really?" she asked. Bassem shot her a glance.

"Is that that what you were thinking?" he asked her.

"Yes."

Basil laughed and shook his head. "Oh Blake, you're so adorable," he said. Bassem looked into the rearview mirror and crossed his eyebrows.

"You have to stop playing jokes on me," said Blake. "Seriously though, what is going to happen to your abductors?"

"Well, Badir will find out who was behind it all and then hand them over to the police. We don't kill people," said Bassem.

"Oh." Blake turned her head and pouted at Basil and then relaxed in her seat. Her heart had been racing thinking about Badir killing those perpetrators, and Basil was just laughing about it. She knew that she needed to play a joke back on him.

It was night when they arrived at Basil's house. Bassem dropped Basil back at his house first before dropping Blake at her place. Blake noticed that his house was heavily guarded. She assumed that it was in response to Basil's abduction.

Blake keyed her address into the navigator for Bassem. He had insisted on driving her home himself. Even though he was driving himself, there was an SUV with a few of his security guards tailing them.

"I'll leave someone to watch over your apartment overnight," Bassem said to Blake when they had arrived at her place.

"Oh, that won't be necessary," she said to him. "I don't think anyone will come looking for me."

Bassem switched off the engine and then turned to face Blake. "My brother's abductors were trying to get to me but got my brother instead," he said softly. Blake raised her eyebrows.

"They wanted you? But why?" she asked. Bassem shrugged his shoulders.

"I am the future king of Al Huddah. That's a big enough reason to make an attempt on my life."

"That's awful."

"They might come after those close to me, since they failed to get to me. So I need you to be safe." He sounded so protective. His masculinity just made Blake's insides melt. She nodded.

"Okay," she said. Bassem reached out and touched her face. He traced her jawline with his finger. Blake was caught off guard by his sudden touch. She felt butterflies fluttering in her stomach. He made her nervous.

Bassem leaned in closer to Blake and gently caressed her lips with his. He placed his thumb against her cheek and held the back of her neck. He pressed his lips against hers and slowly kissed them. Blake closed her eyes and placed her hand on his rock-hard chest. She responded to him by slightly parting her lips and kissing him back.

Bassem's lips felt good against hers. He caressed her jawline with his thumb. The combination was so intense and made Blake not want to let go of him. He was such a good kisser. Blake could feel the kiss all the way down to her toes. She couldn't help but curl them. She had been kissed before but not like that.

He broke off the kiss and pulled away from her. "Call me if something happens," he said to her.

"Huh?" Blake was still so immersed in tangles of passion. It took her a moment to comprehend what he had just said to her. She cleared her throat. "Yes, I will, yeah. Goodnight," she said. She turned to open the door and scrambled out of the car. She almost stumbled on her way out of the car. She straightened her hoodie and then headed to her apartment.

Chapter 14

A few days later, Basil and Bassem were sipping coffee and chatting at Bassem's house in the living room. Basil had come over early for breakfast.

"What's between you and Blake?" Basil asked his brother.

"She works for me," Bassem replied as he flipped through the newspaper. He picked up his coffee and took a sip.

"There is more than that."

"I have no idea what you are talking about."

"I've seen how you look at her." Basil took a bite out of his toast.

"Like a human being?" Bassem's tone was rather sarcastic and Basil caught on. He chuckled a little.

"Like a human being that you have romantic feelings for," he said. Bassem directed his gaze from the newspaper to his brother.

"What are you talking about?"

"I also noticed how you get jealous every time I get close to her," Basil pointed out. Bassem raised an eyebrow. "The moment I kissed her cheek was when you decided that it was time for us to leave. Then you made sure she sat in the front with you," he added.

"I just don't want you flirting with my staff," said Bassem. Basil laughed.

"Then you drove her to her doorstep. When have you ever done that? You've never even done that for your past lovers."

It was true. Bassem drove himself places from time to time. However, he had never taken it upon himself to drive anyone anywhere. When he had dropped Blake off at her house, he had kissed her and it had felt good. Thinking about it again made him want to kiss her. It had only been three days since he had seen her, but it felt much longer. Bassem wondered if his brother was right. Did he have romantic feelings for Blake or not? He hadn't given it much thought.

His thoughts were interrupted by a maid rushing into his living room. "Excuse me, your highnesses, her majesty has arrived," said the maid. Bassem and Basil looked at each other.

"Whose majesty?" Bassem asked as he put the newspaper down. "Mother is here?" he added.

"Yes," the maid replied. Basil sprung up to his feet.

"I can guess why she is here," he said.

A tall, olive-skinned, elegant older woman wearing pearls walked into the room. "Mother," Bassem and

Basil said in chorus. She rushed over to Basil and held his face in her hands.

"Are you alright?" she asked him.

"I'm fine." Basil flashed a grin. She threw her arms around him and held him tightly.

"I'm glad you're okay," she said. She released him from her embrace and then rushed over to her other son. She inspected him before she hugged him. Bassem just stood there with his arms at his sides. He wasn't an affectionate person.

"What brings you here?" Bassem asked. The queen released him from her embrace.

"I obviously came to make sure that the two of you are okay."

"Who told you?" Bassem had been planning to tell his parents about the abduction but hadn't yet. The queen crossed her perfectly threaded eyebrows at him.

"Did you think that you could keep such a secret from your father and me?" she asked.

"I hoped to keep it quiet a few more days," Bassem replied honestly. He wanted to find out who was behind the abduction first.

"That is ridiculous! You should have made us aware the moment it happened," the queen spat out.

"I didn't want to worry you."

The queen placed her hand on her heart. "I could have lost you both," she said. Bassem thought his mother was being hysterical but he could understand where she was coming from.

"This is why I need the both of you to get married and settle down in Al Huddah." She gracefully sat down on one of the sofas and tucked one ankle behind the other. Bassem sat down next to her, and Basil sat down opposite her.

"Even if we were in Al Huddah, someone could still have made an attempt on our lives," said Bassem. His mother shook her head.

"A lot of people are scared of your father. Only a fool would attempt such a fruitless venture in his country," she said. "They probably thought that your father has lesser eyes here and that you would be caught off guard," she added. Bassem sighed heavily.

"We were caught off guard. We had lesser security," he replied.

"From here on, make sure that you are fully protected at all times. I wouldn't be able to live if something happens to either one of you."

"Sometimes having too much security brings more attention," said Basil.

"I don't care. I just want you safe and alive," said the queen.

"How did the king react to the news?" said Bassem.

"He isn't pleased." The queen sighed. "He summoned Badir to the palace."

"Oh lord." Basil shook his head.

"He isn't to blame for this," said Bassem.

"Maybe not, but he is in charge of your security. Your father wants answers," said the queen. Bassem crossed his eyebrows.

"But why Badir didn't say anything?" Bassem wondered.

"He probably hasn't heard yet. The person sent to him left around the same time as I did."

Bassem groaned in response. Knowing his father, Badir was going to be held responsible for Basil getting abducted. The king wouldn't be pleased about him not knowing who was behind it either. Bassem knew that he had to go to Al Huddah before his father summoned him and to speak up for Badir. He was too valuable to him. He couldn't leave him to get punished by the king.

One of the maids walked into the room with some tea for the queen. She took the cup and took a sip. "Just what I needed," she said before she took another sip. She put her cup down and then looked at Basil.

"Have you been staying out of trouble?" the queen asked her younger son.

Basil flashed a mischievous grin.

"Of course," he replied.

"You need a wife." She didn't look convinced.

"Bassem has to get married first since he is older and the crown prince."

Bassem frowned at Basil. The last thing he wanted to talk about was marriage. Basil grinned at Bassem and wiggled his eyebrows. The queen turned her attention to Bassem.

"You definitely need to get married within the next few months. People are starting to talk. They're wondering why there isn't a crown princess," she said to him.

"Then let them wonder," Bassem spat out. He didn't care what people thought of him. The queen raised her eyebrows.

"I have a few women in mind. I'd like for you to meet them."

"Maybe he already has another woman in mind," Basil interjected. Bassem narrowed his gaze at his brother. He knew that Basil was referring to Blake.

"What?" The queen whipped her head in Bassem's direction. "Do you have a lover?" she asked.

"No," Bassem replied, although the idea of making Blake his lover wasn't so bad. She was a very attractive woman. She was smart and beautiful.

"It's okay if you have one. However, if she is a Western woman you know that she can only be a lover. You must marry an Arabic woman."

Basil looked at Bassem with a questioning glare. It was as if he was asking Bassem what he was going to do. Bassem shrugged his shoulders and looked at his mother.

"I don't have a lover," he said to her.

"You were always too serious. There is nothing wrong with you having a woman."

Bassem rose to his feet. "I have matters to attend to. When I return, we'll head for the airport," he said to his mother.

"The airport?" she asked.

"We are going to Al Huddah tonight."

"You're going to see father?" Basil asked.

"You're coming too." Bassem kissed his mother on the cheek.

"Why am I coming?"

"I am sure father would like to see us both. We might as well go before he calls for us." Bassem also needed Basil to be with him and not with Blake. He knew that if his brother stayed behind in Austin, he would linger around Blake. He didn't want the two of them getting any closer than they already were.

Chapter 15

Bassem arrived at the building site for his new home. There were builders everywhere already digging and drilling. Before they had started working on his land, he had got his secretary to look into their backgrounds. Everyone he worked with needed to have an impeccable profile and pass a background check. Even though Blake had vouched for them, Bassem needed to be sure.

The sheikh opened the car door and stepped out of the expensive vehicle. He marched towards the building site for a quick inspection before he departed for Al Huddah. He had already spoken to his secretary and given her orders on things he needed her to take care of while he was gone.

As Bassem was walking towards the building site, he saw Blake speaking with one of the construction workers. It was the first time he was seeing her since they kissed. Even though he had enjoyed the taste of her lips, he needed to back off. He had concluded that it was a bad idea getting involved with one of his workers. He needed all his romantic attachments to not be involved in his daily life because usually he lost interest quickly and didn't want to have to deal with the woman after that. He just wanted them gone and out of his life.

"Miss Gordon," he said as he approached Blake. She turned around and looked at him. Her green eyes lit up.

"Good afternoon, sheikh," she greeted him. For a few seconds they just stared at each other. No one said anything. Seeing her curvy body and luscious lips again made Bassem want to pull her into his arms. However, he had to suppress that urge.

"Who is he?" Bassem gestured towards the man Blake had been speaking to. He had to say something to cut the tension that was growing between them.

"Oh." Blake cleared her throat. "This is Lenny. He is a builder and the man in charge." Blake touched Lenny's shoulder and smiled at him. Lenny smiled back at her. Bassem raised an eyebrow. They seemed rather close.

"Pleasure to meet you, sir," Lenny said to Bassem.

"I hope this project runs smoothly. I look forward to moving into my house sometime this year," said Bassem. Lenny laughed nervously.

"It's a short time."

"I'm sure you can do it, *Lenny*." Bassem frowned a little when he said his name.

"I will do my best, sir."

"Could you give Miss Gordon and me some privacy?" Bassem asked, even though he really wanted to tell him to just go away.

"Yes," Lenny replied. He looked at Blake and touched her shoulder. "I will speak to you later," he said to her before he walked off. Blake smiled and nodded. Bassem frowned a little. There was no need for *Lenny* to touch Blake's shoulder. There was no need for him to touch her anywhere.

"What kind of a name is Lenny anyway?" Bassem mumbled after he had left.

"Excuse me?" said Blake.

"How is everything going here?"

"It's going well. We started drilling on Monday. Tomorrow we should be able to start building the foundation," she said. Bassem nodded.

"I am leaving for Al Huddah tonight."

"You are?"

Bassem slipped his hands in his pockets. "If you need anything, contact my secretary," he said.

"Sure. How long will you be gone for?" Blake laced her fingers together.

"I'm not sure yet," Bassem replied. Blake nodded. The wind whispered through Blake's wavy brunette locks, revealing her silky fair skin. Bassem could remember how soft her skin had felt against his fingertips. She looked down shyly and tucked a lock of hair behind her ear. Blake looked up and slightly bit her bottom lip. Her plump, pale pink lips were inviting. Bassem closed his eyes momentarily to ward off the temptation.

"Okay then." Bassem turned sharply and started walking back to his car.

"Have a good journey!" Blake called out behind him but he didn't respond. He just had to get away from her. He was always good at controlling himself around women but he was suddenly finding it hard around Blake. He just wanted to hold her and kiss her.

***

Blake kicked off her shoes and threw herself on the sofa when she arrived home. It had been a long day. She had been busy. She had had so many things to do and supervise. However, the only thing that she was thinking about was Bassem. Her heart had doubled over in her chest when she had seen him. She so badly wanted to wrap her arms around him and press her lips to his but she hadn't.

It had been the first time that they had seen each other since they had kissed. Blake didn't know what she had been expecting but it wasn't that. Bassem had acted as though he had no recollection of the kiss. Blake felt a sharp pain in her heart when she remembered how he had left. He had just walked away in the middle of the conversation. He couldn't wait to get away from her. He probably regretted kissing her. Blake squealed in embarrassment.

The doorbell rang and interrupted her squealing and self-pity. She rose to her feet and headed for the door. She opened it and found CJ standing there.

"Perfect timing," said Blake. She turned and headed back to the living room.

"Why?" CJ shut the door behind herself and rushed after Blake.

"I feel weird."

"Because you are weird." CJ burst into laughter, but Blake didn't. She just stared at her with a blank facial expression. "Sorry, what's the matter?" CJ cleared her throat.

"I told you that Bassem brought me home after we went to find Basil."

"Yeah?"

"However, I didn't tell you that Bassem kissed me."

CJ's eyebrows shot up into her forehead. "What?" she spat out. She quickly sat down on the sofa next to Blake. "Tell me everything," she said. Blake shrugged her shoulders.

"The first time he kissed me was actually in the woods before he went out to get Basil. He just gave me a quick kiss as if it were something that we normally did," Blake explained. CJ curled her upper lip.

"And you waited this long to tell me because?"

"It's only been three days."

"That is long to me."

Blake rolled her eyes. "Then when he drove me home, he kissed me before I left the car." Blake's cheeks turned red as she remembered that night. She could still remember the softness of his lips, and the silkiness of his fingertips tracing her jawline.

"Was he a good kisser?" CJ asked. Her question didn't even shock Blake. Her friend was always too forward. Blake rolled her eyes and leaned her head against the sofa.

"Yes," she replied. She had never been kissed like that. She was sure she was going to remember that kiss for a long time.

"I'm not surprised. I knew he would make a good lover."

"He came to the construction site today."

"And?" CJ's eyes widened with excitement.

"And nothing." Blake pouted.

"What does that mean?" CJ frowned.

"We had a short and awkward conversation. He basically came to check on the construction and to just let me know that he was leaving for Al Huddah."

"He didn't pull you into his arms and claim your lips with his?"

"Cora, this isn't a movie." Blake shook her head as she sprang up to her feet and headed for the kitchen.

"Did he at least say something cheesy like I missed you or I want you?" CJ asked as she followed Blake to the kitchen.

"No." Blake opened the fridge and pulled out a frozen pizza. She didn't feel like cooking. She just wanted something that required no effort to make.

"Huh? I'm confused. He didn't try to flirt with you or anything?" CJ heaved herself up onto the kitchen counter.

"No he didn't. There was no flirting. He was acting as though nothing happened. He was probably regretting it." Blake peeled off the cover and put the pizza in the oven.

"Will you confront him about it?"

"No." Blake turned the oven on. She heaved herself up onto the white kitchen counter. "What would I say?" she asked.

"Get straight to the point. 'Do you regret kissing me?'"

"Ha!" Blake burst into laughter. "I don't want to hear the answer to that."

"So what will you do?"

"Act like nothing happened and just do my job."

CJ raised an eyebrow. "That is a bad idea," she said.

"It's actually a good idea," Blake replied. CJ sighed.

"I guess you can wait to see what he says or does. Then judging from how he's acting you can decide whether you want to confront him about it, move on or kiss him again."

"I am not going to initiate a kiss!" The thought of it made Blake shy.

"You're such a chicken," CJ teased.

"I don't care, I will not do it." Blake laughed. CJ laughed with her.

"This pizza needs to hurry up and cook. I am starving," she said. CJ was always inviting herself over for meals. Blake was used to it.

"Me too," Blake replied.

Chapter 16

Bassem arrived at the palace on Thursday morning. He rushed to his quarters to freshen up before he went to meet the king. The king may have been his father but that didn't mean he didn't have to take care of his appearance before he met with him. Basil went to his quarters to get ready also.

The two brothers reunited in front of the king's quarters half an hour later. One of the palace guards outside the king's quarters opened the doors for them. Bassem walked in first. Basil followed a few steps behind him. The king was sitting at the breakfast table about to start eating when Bassem and Basil arrived. A maid announced their arrival as they walked into the dining room.

"I knew you would come, but not this early," the king said as he unfolded his napkin.

"Good morning, Father," Bassem and Basil said in chorus as they bowed their heads. A maid poured black coffee into a cup for the king.

"Bring plates and cutlery for the princes," the king instructed her.

"Yes, your majesty." She bowed her head and then left the room.

"Have a seat," the king said to Bassem and Basil. The brothers joined their father at the breakfast table. The maid walked back into the room and served them their food.

The king ate his eggs quietly. Bassem knew his father was really angry. Whenever he took his time to tell them off, that was when he was most angry.

"Sheikh Khalifar," the king said quietly.

"Pardon?" Bassem replied. The king wiped his mouth with a napkin.

"Sheikh Khalifar was behind the abduction."

Basil and Bassem looked at each other and then at the king. "You found out already?" Bassem asked.

"Of course I did. He was after you as his competitor and the crown prince of Al Huddah," the king explained. Bassem knew Sheikh Khalifar. He was Bassem's number one competitor. He owned an oil business also. The sheikh was from a neighboring country.

"That was a careless move on his part." Bassem shook his head.

"It was careless and reckless for you not to tell me."

"I was going to tell you."

"When?" The king shot him an icy gaze.

"I wanted to find out who was behind it first."

118

"It's my fault for not being careful," said Basil. The king looked at him.

"When will you grow up? You are just playing around in Austin and wasting money," the king said to him. Basil opened his mouth and then closed it. "From now onwards, you will work as one of the geologists in Austin and Dallas," the king added.

"But Father—" Before Basil could protest, the king cut him off with his hand.

"It's either that or I freeze your assets." The king paused for a moment. "Actually, I will freeze your assets. Your spending money will be your salary," he added.

"That is a bit harsh, Father," said Bassem. The king turned to face him.

"As for you, you will meet with Keira. She is Sheikh Mirak's eldest daughter. That is whom your mother and I have agreed on being our daughter-in-law."

"I am not ready to wed."

"That was not a suggestion."

"Yes, your majesty." Bassem knew it was pointless to try and disagree with his father. He was not going to win the argument.

"You are thirty years old and the crown prince. You should have been married years ago." The king rubbed the temples of his head. "I will take Badir's resignation."

Bassem's eyes flew wide open. "You want to fire him?" he asked.

"It's a small price to pay for this situation."

"The abduction was not his fault."

"When I sent him to Austin with you, it was under the assumption that he was good at his job and that he was going to protect the both of you. He failed at that."

"He found Basil no more than twenty-four hours later," said Bassem.

"Anything could have happened within those hours. Do you understand the magnitude of your error?"

"I do, Father. Please don't let Badir pay for it. He is the only man I trust with my life," Bassem replied. Bassem had found that the men that had kidnapped Basil had been hired to do so. They were petty criminals that had been paid for the kidnapping.

"The only reason that I am even considering letting him keep his job is because he found the person that stole the van. That man had been paid a handsome amount a few days before. My men then traced the payment back to Youssef Hadid," said the king.

"Youssef Hadid; Sheikh Khalifar's nephew and right-hand man," said Bassem. His face darkened. The king rose from his seat.

"You may keep Badir but he will get a pay cut and his land seized, and you will marry Keira," he said to Bassem. Basil and Bassem immediately rose to their feet and bowed their heads to the king.

"Yes, your majesty," Bassem replied. The king walked out of the room. Basil exhaled loudly and sat down. "That wasn't too bad," said Bassem as he sat down. Basil raised his eyebrow.

"What are you talking about? I have to work as a geologist," he complained.

"You are qualified enough."

Basil frowned. "Do you know how little the salary is?" Basil shuddered. Bassem took a sip of his coffee. He knew why his father was making Basil work a regular job. He wanted to discipline him and wanted him to learn about hard work and the true value of money. Basil had never wanted to learn about the family business. He just spent money on fast cars and women.

"I pity you on that," said Bassem. "At least you don't have to get married," he added.

"What will you do about Blake?"

121

"There is nothing to do about her." She was not his woman. So why would he need to do anything about her?

"I am disappointed in you." Basil shook his head.

"Why?" Bassem asked dryly.

"I thought you had finally met a woman you could love but instead you are going to deny your feelings and just go along with what father says."

Bassem raised his eyebrows. Part of him felt saddened by the idea of not pursuing anything with Blake. "We only shared a kiss. That doesn't mean that I have feelings for her," he said. Basil raised his eyebrows.

"You kissed her?" he asked. He looked so amused.

"Yes."

"And?"

"And what?"

"What was it like? Do you crave her?"

"I am not having this conversation with you."

"Then with who? It's not like you open up to anyone else." Basil took a bite of his toast.

"It was just a kiss. I didn't make a big deal out of it and neither should you." Bassem sipped his coffee and then rose to his feet. "I have to go and get ready to meet Keira," he said and then headed for the exit.

"My stone-cold brother!" Basil called out after him. Bassem just ignored him and kept walking away.

***

Bassem headed downstairs after a maid told him that Keira had arrived. He had changed into a white shirt and a pair of grey trousers. He didn't know what was appropriate or inappropriate when meeting with a betrothed. So, he decided to dress as he normally did.

He walked out into the palace where an unfamiliar woman waited for him in a courtyard. She was sitting at a marble-topped table and rose to her feet when Bassem walked out. He studied her as he walked towards her. She was tall, probably about five feet nine inches. She was slim but curvy. She wore a beige dress that complemented her bronze skin. Her jet-black hair was tied up into a neat ponytail.

"Your highness," she said with a curtsy when Bassem approached her. She wore small diamond earrings. She had an impressive bone structure.

"You must be Keira," said Bassem.

Chapter 17

Keira and Bassem sat down at the table. Bassem leaned back into his chair and studied her even further. She was a beautiful woman. She had a perfectly straight nose and high cheekbones. He could see why his mother had chosen her for him.

"It's great to finally meet you," she said to him. Her voice was as smooth as honey.

"Why?" Bassem asked.

"I have heard so much about you and I've long admired you. I just wanted to meet you in person."

"Why do you admire me?"

"You graduated at the top of your class at MIT. Your grades were among the highest in the country."

"So because I am intelligent?" Bassem asked. Keira smiled and shook her head.

"Your family business has improved by 6% since you moved to Austin. You are quite intelligent and hardworking," she replied. Bassem barely reacted.

"You've been keeping an eye on me."

Keira laughed softly. A maid walked out onto the courtyard and brought them refreshments. She bowed her head before she disappeared. Keira took it upon herself to pick up a glass of cold juice and hand it to the sheikh. Bassem took the glass from her and took a sip.

"What do you hope to gain from this marriage?" he asked her.

"Your heart," she replied. Bassem let out a laugh. She was definitely trying her best to charm him.

"Let's talk about something achievable," he said. Every woman he had been with always talked about gaining his heart. Bassem didn't concern himself with such frivolous things. And if he did, he had never met a woman that was worth getting his *heart*. They were all so shallow and boring.

"I believe that is achievable. I am a determined woman," she said.

"It'll be a waste of your energy."

"It'll be worth it."

Bassem raised his eyebrows. "How old are you?" he asked her.

"Twenty-seven."

"Why aren't you married?"

"The right man hadn't come along, and I believe that he has now."

Bassem narrowed his gaze. "Flattery doesn't work with me," he said. There was no need for her to try so hard. The king had already ordered Bassem to marry her.

"I am just being honest, your highness," Keira replied. Bassem just sighed and took a sip of his drink. He put his glass down and then rose to his feet.

"We have reached the end of our meeting," he said. Keira rose from her seat.

"Already?" She looked confused. "We haven't finished talking."

"What more is there to talk about?"

"We need to get to know each other."

Bassem shrugged his shoulders. "We shall leave that for another time," he said. He turned on his heel and walked off. His father had demanded that he meet with Keira and he had done so.

***

Blake was sitting in her living room watching TV when the doorbell rang. She jumped off the sofa and ran to the front door. She opened it expecting CJ but she was wrong.

"Basil?" She was surprised to see the sheikh's brother at her doorstep. "How did you even know where I live?"

"Do you think a man of my status wouldn't be able to find out where you live?" he asked.

"That's creepy." Blake shrugged her shoulders. "Come in."

"Thanks." Basil walked into her apartment. "I brought churros and ice cream."

"Oh yay. I like churros," she said as they entered the living room.

"I thought you would."

They sat down at the sofas and started eating. "So, what brought you over?" Blake asked him.

"Well, it's Sunday and I thought you would be home. I just wanted to come over and say hello," he replied. Blake raised an eyebrow.

"Did your brother give you my address?" Blake wanted to ask him about Bassem but she didn't want to be so obvious.

"No. He's still in Al Huddah."

"Still?"

"He told you he was leaving?"

"Yes." Blake nodded.

"I returned last night but he stayed behind because he had some matters to attend to. He should be returning within a day or two."

Blake was not sure how she felt about seeing Bassem. It had been awkward the last time they had met. Part of her wanted to see him but she was worried about how it was going to be. She had told herself that she was not going to develop any feelings for him and yet she found herself thinking about him more than she needed to.

"Oh I see," Blake replied. "Do your parents know about the abduction?"

"Funny you mention that."

"Why?"

Basil explained to Blake that when their mother found out, she came to Austin immediately. Then they returned to Al Huddah because it was only a matter of time until their father summoned them. He told her about the king making Basil work and live on his salary. Blake couldn't help but laugh.

"Geologists make a lot of money," she said. Basil curled his upper lip.

"It's not enough for me to live on," he complained. Blake rolled her eyes.

"I have no sympathy for you. I've had to live on part-time jobs that pay much less than a geologist when I was at the university."

"Have you?"

"Of course. I actually attended MIT on scholarship."

"Wow, you must have been very smart. MIT is already hard to get into, but getting a scholarship;

that's impressive," he said before stuffing a churro into his mouth.

"I just worked very hard." Blake smiled.

"Did you know that Bassem went to MIT?"

Blake looked surprised. "I didn't know that," she admitted.

"He did, and he did very well."

"He's smart?"

Basil nodded. "He is the most intelligent man in our family," he said.

"What about you?"

Basil smiled. "Of course I am intelligent, I am just lazy and not interested in the family business," he replied. Blake swallowed her ice cream.

"Why aren't you interested?" she asked.

"It's not my thing."

"Then what is your *thing*?"

"Parties, clubs, jewelry, cars, women." Basil grinned. Blake rolled her eyes. He was so different to his brother.

"You deserve getting your assets frozen."

"That's not fair," Basil complained. Blake laughed.

"You might enjoy it, you never know," she said. Basil just pouted in response. The two of them watched TV and talked about random things.

***

On Tuesday, Blake was at the office dealing with some paperwork. She decided to go check on the construction site. She had to make sure everything was moving along perfectly. Bassem had made it clear that he wanted his house to be completed as soon as possible without any mistakes.

Blake parked her car and opened the door. As she was walking, she noticed a tall man with a broad back. He was wearing charcoal trousers and a navy blue shirt. He had his hands in his pockets, and he was talking to one of the construction workers. Blake's stomach knotted up. She knew who it was. It was Bassem.

She thought about turning around and getting back in her car, but her plan was spoiled when the construction worker saw her. "Miss Gordon!" he yelled out. Bassem turned his head and immediately made eye contact with Blake. She awkwardly forced a smile and approached them.

"Hello, Sheikh Sedarous," she said. Bassem kept looking at her.

"Hello Blake," he said. Blake inhaled sharply. That was the first time that he had called her by her first name. Her name sounded beautiful on his lips. His deep voice was so smooth and seductive. Blake didn't know what to say or do, so she just stared at him. And he stared back.

Chapter 18

It felt as though there as though there was no one else but Blake and Bassem. It was strange how much this man affected her. She had known him for a very short time and yet he was having such an effect on her. She didn't know what to say or do. Her gaze was just fixed on him. She wanted him to hold and kiss her. She wanted to know that the kiss they had shared wasn't a mistake.

"Um, Miss Gordon?" the construction worker interrupted Blake and Bassem's moment.

"Yes." Blake cleared her throat and looked at him.

"Are you okay?"

"Yes, I am. I am fine." Blake forced a smile. She was not okay.

"The sheikh was just checking up on our progress."

"Ah." Blake nodded. "I just came to do so myself. I was at the office. I had some paperwork to deal with."

"I see," Bassem replied.

"Yeah. Um, how was your trip to Al Huddah?"

"Fine." He was being cold. Why was he being cold to her? Blake wanted to ask him but she was too much of a coward. She was scared that he would tell her that it was only one kiss and that she shouldn't make a big deal out of it. He probably had more women.

"Good," Blake snapped.

"Yes," Bassem replied.

"Sheikh Sedarous," Lenny said as he approached. "It's good to see you again."

"Hello Lenny." Bassem slightly frowned. "Is that short for something?"

"Leonard, but I don't mind Lenny." He smiled.

"Leonard sounds better."

Lenny laughed awkwardly. He turned his attention to Blake. "I didn't know you were coming today." He touched her shoulder.

"I will be coming on most days," she said.

"Okay, I have matters to attend to," said Bassem.

"Have a good day," Blake said to him. She felt a little bit of anger inside of her. He was leaving without really speaking to her. There was no "it was nice to see you" or "how are you" or even a smile.

"I hope to see you soon," said Lenny. Bassem didn't respond. He just turned on his heel and walked off. Blake watched him walking off. He confidently strode off without a care in the world. Blake crossed her arms over her chest and pouted. Why was he being like that to her?

"Blake!" she heard Lenny call out. Blake turned and looked at him.

"What?" she snapped.

"Didn't you hear me speaking to you?"

"No, what's wrong?"

"Nothing is wrong. I just wanted to show you what we did yesterday and today."

"Oh, please show me," she replied. Lenny nodded and began walking. Blake walked off with him. Blake fished her cell phone out of her bag and took photos of their work. She liked to keep very detailed records of her projects. She scribbled a few notes down. Lenny talked to her and tried to make a few jokes but she wasn't in the mood. All she could think about was Bassem.

***

"Good afternoon, sheikh," Amina greeted Bassem as he walked past her desk. Bassem grunted in response and just kept heading to his office. There was nothing good about the afternoon.

Bassem walked into his office and slammed the door behind him. He sat in his chair at his desk. Lenny was so annoying, Bassem thought to himself. He didn't like seeing Lenny around Blake. He seemed to flirt with her a little too much. And the problem was that Blake didn't ward him off. She just smiled at him.

Blake looked so beautiful. She was wearing a high-waisted skirt that showed off her beautiful curves. Why was she still on his mind? Bassem couldn't understand why he was still thinking about her. It was unlike like him to be so fixated on a woman. What was happening to him? He was getting married in a couple of months. He needed to forget about Blake.

A knock sounded on the door. "I'm busy!" Bassem called out. He couldn't be bothered to deal with anyone or anything. The door swung open anyway and Basil walked in.

"Good afternoon, sir," he said as he walked in. Bassem raised an eyebrow.

"What are you up to now?"

"Nothing mischievous." Basil pulled out the chair from Bassem's desk and sat down opposite him. "I've been working here since yesterday," he said.

"What?" Bassem had no idea what his brother was talking about.

"I have to work as a geologist, remember?" Basil frowned.

"Oh." Bassem laughed a little. "It's a good job. What is the problem?"

"I have to live on that salary. That isn't fair."

"I'm actually surprised that it took father this long to make you work in the company. He has always been displeased with your partying and lack of responsibility."

Basil frowned. "I don't want to work in the family company though," he said.

"You have to work somewhere. You can't just party for the rest of your life. Be grateful, there are people that have a lot less in life," he replied. Basil curled his upper lip.

"You and Blake think alike."

"Why are you bringing up Blake here?" Bassem snapped.

"She also thinks that father wasn't extreme with his punishment and that being a geologist is a good job."

Bassem raised his eyebrows. "You've met with Blake?" he asked.

"Yes." Basil smiled.

"When?" Bassem didn't return his smile. What business did Basil have with Blake? There was no reason for them to be meeting up.

"Over the weekend," Basil replied.

"Why?"

"Easy with the questions."

"There is no reason for you to be meeting up with her. What did you talk about?"

"We are friends. We can meet up whenever we feel like it. Besides, why does it matter to you whether we do so or not?" Basil looked at his brother suspiciously.

"I told you that I didn't want you have romantic attachments with any of my workers."

"You're particularly sensitive when it comes to Miss Gordon," Basil replied. Bassem crossed his eyebrows.

"No, I'm not," he spat out. "Why are you here anyway? I am kind of busy."

"Why are you so stubborn? Clearly you have feeling for Blake."

"I don't." The words didn't sound convincing to Bassem. He said that he didn't have feelings for her but he didn't believe himself whenever he said it. "I'm getting married in two months," he added.

"As if you want to," said Basil.

"I have no choice."

"At least, Keira is a beautiful woman."

"You've seen her before?"

"Yes, I have."

"Where?"

"Relax, I've not been romantically involved with her or anyone close to her," said Basil. Bassem was glad to hear it. He didn't want rumors that involved his brother and his future wife to start floating about.

"She's very eager to marry me," said Bassem. When he had met her, she was so smiley and mentioned how he was the right man for her. She had called his phone that very night and the day after.

"I'm sure a lot of women are very eager to be your wife," said Basil. "I know many women want me. We look the same, so you must be having the same problem."

Bassem shook his head at his brother's vanity. "It's not about looks. It's mostly about money and power," he said.

"That too."

"She called my phone."

"How does she have your number?"

"Mother gave it to her of course."

Basil shook his head. "She's so eager for us to settle down," he said.

"Keira isn't a bad-looking woman. She just needs to be less eager, and she talks too much. I don't want a wife that talks too much," said Bassem.

"She's not Blake."

"Of course she's not Blake. They're two different women."

"That's not what I mean."

"I don't care what you mean."

"You're not attracted to Keira but you're going to marry her anyway." Basil rose to his feet. "If you're not going to make a move on Blake, then leave her to me," he added. Bassem sprang up to his feet.

"Stay away from her," he warned. Basil raised his eyebrows and looked at his brother from head to toe. He looked amused. He turned and headed out of Bassem's office without saying a word.

Chapter 19

Blake took it upon herself to go to Bassem's office and update him on their project. It was the end of the week, and Bassem hadn't been to the construction site since Tuesday. They had made a lot of progress, and she was going to need more funds. He had told her to go through his secretary but she needed an excuse to meet up with him.

"Is the sheikh expecting you?" Amina asked Blake as she approached her desk.

"Yes. It's just a quick meeting. It won't be long." Blake smiled at Amina and headed for the sheikh's office.

"I don't think that's a good idea." Amina rushed after Blake.

"Is he meeting with someone?"

"No but at least let me call him and ask if it's alright for you to go in."

Blake stopped right in front of Bassem's office. She took a deep breath and then knocked on the door.

"Come in," Bassem called out. Blake turned the door and walked into his office. Bassem was sitting at his desk with some paperwork. He looked up and saw Blake and Amina walking in.

"I tried to stop her," said Amina. She looked nervous.

"It's okay," Bassem replied. He looked good, Blake thought to herself. His beard had been trimmed down. It looked about a week old. His hair was neatly brushed as usual. He wore a black shirt and burgundy trousers.

Amina bowed her head and walked out of the room. Blake slowly approached Bassem's desk. He gestured for her to sit down. Blake sat down at the chair opposite him.

"What brings you to my office?" Bassem asked her.

"Work," Blake replied. She was a little bit annoyed by the fact that he hadn't even greeted her or asked how she was. "I came to show you the progress on your house," she added.

"Show me?"

"I have photos." She pulled out a file with the photos and put them on the desk.

"You could have e-mailed them to my secretary."

He really had no interest in seeing her, she thought to herself. "I also wanted to ask for more funds. We needed more materials," she said.

"You have my accountant's number," he said in an icy tone. Blake swallowed nervously. Why had

Bassem changed so much? How could he kiss her and just act as though nothing had happened?

"I guess there is no reason for us to meet then," she said to him. He didn't respond. He just leaned back in his chair and kept his gaze on her. His stare was so intense, it made Blake very nervous. She sprang up to her feet and turned on her heel. She headed for the door. She turned the doorknob and walked out.

She chastised herself as she headed for the elevator. It was her fault for coming over unannounced. It was her fault for not getting the hint. She had met him twice since then, and he hadn't showed any interest in her. She should have just left him alone.

"Are you okay?" a voice interrupted her thoughts.

"What?" Blake turned to see Basil standing next to her.

"You are pressing that button so hard. What did it do to you?"

Blake looked at the elevator button and removed her finger. She had been so engrossed in her thoughts that she hadn't realized that she was poking it so hard. "The elevator is taking forever to come," she said. Basil raised an eyebrow.

"Were you here to see my brother?" he asked.

"Yes." Blake placed her hands on her hips and started tapping her foot.

"Things didn't go well?"

"Why is he so cold?" She whipped her head in Basil's direction and waited for an answer.

"That's how he is," Basil replied carefully.

"Why did I even bother coming here?" She crossed her arms over her chest. "Why is the elevator taking so long to come?" she snapped.

"Blake, what's going on? Do you want to talk about it?" Basil said gently.

"Yes."

"Okay, let's go to my office."

"Not to you." She turned around and marched towards Bassem's office. Basil was just left by the elevator speechless.

"Are you going in there again?" Amina asked as she sprang up to her feet.

"Yes," Blake replied as she walked past Amina. She swung Bassem's door open and shut it behind her. Bassem raised his eyebrows.

"Did you forget something?" he asked.

"I learned the first time that keeping quiet didn't help me at all," she said to him.

"I am confused. What is this about?"

"You kissed me." She went straight to the point. Bassem stared at her with an unreadable expression. "I didn't make that move, you did," she added.

"I did." Bassem frowned. He was probably wondering where she was going with her words. Blake didn't know either. She was just saying whatever came to her mind. He had made such an impact on her. She wasn't the woman to lose her calm. She was acting out of character because of Bassem. She liked him so much and it was driving her crazy that he was avoiding her so much.

"This is just so unfair," she said. His short answer made her nervous. She needed him to say more to her. She needed something.

"What is?"

"This! You!"

"Blake." There it was again. Bassem had called her by her first name. Hearing him say her name made her almost melt like butter in a hot pan. "You are not making sense," he said.

"No, you are not making sense," she said. Bassem raised his eyebrows. He slowly got up from his seat. "You just kissed me and then we never talked about it. You just decided to act like nothing happened. Your actions aren't making sense," she added. Bassem walked around the table. The closer he got to Blake, the more nervous she grew. She lost her resolve. So she turned and rushed out of his office.

She got into the elevator and headed to the ground floor. As soon as the doors opened, she walked out and headed to her car. Blake chastised herself for going back to his office. She hadn't gained anything. She still didn't have an answer for his actions. She felt so stupid for going back into his office and making a fool out of herself.

Blake arrived at her apartment not too long after. She frowned as she walked into her apartment. She could smell cooked food. "Hello!" she called out. She followed the smell to her kitchen. She saw her mother and CJ in the kitchen.

"Mom?" she said.

"Blakie!" the older woman cried out as she quickly approached her. She wrapped her arms around her. Her mother was a head shorter. Blake had gotten her height from her father. She hugged her mother tightly and kissed her on top of her head.

"When did you get here?" Blake asked her.

"About an hour ago. CJ let me in," she said. CJ smiled at Blake. She had a key to Blake's apartment, which she was meant to use in an emergency.

"Why didn't you tell me that my mother was here?" Blake asked CJ.

"I told her not to. I wanted to surprise you," said her mother.

"This house is so clean," Aunt Moira said as she walked into the kitchen. Blake's eyes widened. She hadn't seen her mother's sister in such a long time.

"Aunt Moira!" Blake quickly hugged her.

"Hey sweetie." Her aunt rubbed her back.

"It's good to see you."

"It's good to see you too, darling." Her aunt was just the same height as her mother. Both of them had long, thick, brunette hair. That was where Blake got it from.

"Let's catch up over dinner. Go set the table," Blake's mother said to her. Blake nodded. She grabbed some dishes and cutlery and went to set the dining table which was just a few feet from the kitchen.

"I'm coming from Bassem's office," Blake whispered to CJ.

"What happened?" CJ placed a fork on the table and then moved closer to Blake.

"I gave him a piece of my mind," she whispered. She didn't want her mother and aunt to hear her. The two of them had always been nagging her about getting a boyfriend. They even tried to set her up with a family friend and it didn't work out.

"You did?" CJ cried out.

"Not really."

CJ frowned at Blake. "Then what?" she asked.

"I just said to him that it wasn't fair. He kissed me and then acted as though it never happened."

"What did he say to that?" CJ looked so excited.

"I walked out before he could say much," Blake replied. CJ's face dropped. Before she could say anything, the doorbell rang.

"It must be delivery. I ordered dessert," said CJ. She dashed out of the kitchen. Blake finished up setting the table.

"Put this casserole dish on the table," her mother said to her. Blake walked through the arched door and into the kitchen. She took the dish from her mother. CJ walked back into the kitchen.

"Blake, it's for you," said CJ. Blake almost dropped the casserole dish when she saw her visitor.

Chapter 20

Blake swallowed nervously. "What are you doing here?" she asked. CJ had her hands on her hips, her gaze shifting between Blake and her visitor.

"I came to see you," said Bassem.

"Who is the handsome gentleman?" Blake's mother asked.

"Is this your boyfriend?" Aunt Moira asked Blake.

"No." Blake gave CJ the casserole dish.

"I'm Bassem Sedarous," Bassem introduced himself. He offered his hand to Blake's mother. She shook his hand with a big smile on her face.

"Hello Bassem." Aunt Moira eyed him up from head to toe as she shook his hand. "Firm grip," she pointed out.

"Excuse us." Blake took Bassem's arm and led him down the hall to her bedroom. The living room was across the kitchen. If she took him in there, her family would hear their conversation. She didn't want that.

"Is this your bedroom?" Bassem asked as he walked in.

"Yes." Blake was grateful that her bedroom was neat and tidy. She had actually changed her sheets and bed covers that very morning. Bassem stood in the middle of her bedroom with his hands in his pockets as he looked around. "Why are you here?" she asked him.

"I think our conversation earlier wasn't finished," he said. Blake narrowed her gaze at him.

"I think it was," she said. Bassem raised an eyebrow.

"You left before I could even say anything to you."

"It didn't seem like you wanted to say anything. You were just so cold and unbothered." Blake laced her fingers together. Her day had started off plain and normal. Now it was just weird and spiraling out of control. First she had made a fool out of herself in front of Bassem. Now he was standing in her bedroom with her mother and aunt down the hall.

"It was amusing seeing you like that."

Blake frowned. "It was amusing? I was nervous and acting out of character all because of you and you found that funny?" she spat out. Bassem held her waist and pulled her closer to him. Blake squeaked as she was suddenly pulled. Her hands landed on his chest.

Before she could register what was happening, Bassem had covered her lips with his. He kissed her so fast and passionately. This kiss was different to the first one. This kiss was more demanding and ungenerous. It left Blake breathless and confused.

Her heart was beating so fast. It took her a moment to come back to her senses.

"You can't do this to me again. You can't come to my house and kiss me and act like nothing happened. Stop playing with my emotions," she said to him.

"That wasn't my intention." Bassem caressed her face with the back of his hand. "I'm not good at these things."

"What things?"

"Relationships, emotions."

Blake laughed a little. Bassem was such a strange man. "So, what are you saying to me right now?" she asked. Bassem searched her eyes before he replied. As he opened his mouth to speak, there was a knock on the door. CJ opened the door and walked in with her hands over her eyes.

"Are you fully clothed?" she teased. Blake released herself from Bassem's embrace and took a few steps back.

"Very funny, Cora," Blake replied. CJ laughed and then uncovered her eyes.

"Your mother set up a place at the table for the sheikh."

"He's not staying for dinner."

"Why not?" Bassem asked. He headed for the door and walked out. Blake watched him with her jaw hung open. She just knew that her mother and aunt would attack him with a thousand questions. It was going to be an uncomfortable dinner.

"What happened in here?" CJ asked.

"I don't know myself," Blake replied honestly. She was still very confused. She headed out of the room and went to the dining table.

They all sat down at the dining table. Her mother, aunt and best friend were all staring at Bassem.

"Mom, Aunt Moira, Bassem is my client," said Blake.

"Is that how you met?" Aunt Moira asked.

"Yes ma'am," Bassem replied. Blake's mother served Bassem and then passed him the plate. "Thank you," he said to her.

"Such a handsome and polite young man. Are you married?" Aunt Moira asked him.

"No, I am not yet married."

"Are you seeing someone?"

He looked at Blake. "Yes I am," he replied. Blake raised her eyebrows. Was he referring to her or not? He was such a strange man. She couldn't guess what he was thinking about.

"Blakie?" her mother asked.

"This tastes really good," said Bassem after tasting the chicken.

"I'm glad you like it. Eat as much as you want."

"What was Blake like growing up?"

Blake looked up from her plate. Why was Bassem asking that? "Let's not talk about that," said Blake.

"She has always been quiet, sweet and intelligent," said her mother.

"In other words, I was a boring child."

"Well, you did hit one boy that was harassing me in the tenth grade," said CJ.

"That was the first time she ever got in trouble at school." Aunt Moira laughed. Bassem looked at Blake with his eyebrows raised.

"She may be quiet, but she speaks when she needs to," said her mother.

"Yes, she told me off today," said Bassem. Blake narrowed her gaze at him. Was he teasing her? She had barely gotten all the words out. She had run away like a coward.

"What did you do to her?"

"Nothing, let's just eat," said Blake.

Blake's mother and aunt asked Bassem all sorts of questions. They wanted to know what he did, what he liked and disliked. They asked his opinion on things. They were so nosy but it paid off. It allowed Blake to learn more about Bassem. The more she heard about him, the more she thought he was amazing.

Blake walked Bassem out after dinner. It was strange how normal it felt. He got along with her mother and aunt so easily. He seemed to enjoy their cooking and company. Blake could tell that they liked him too. Her mother had actually packed him some food to take home.

"You must think that my family is weird," Blake said to Bassem.

"No." He shook his head. "They're just different to my family."

"Is that good or bad?"

"It's good." They stopped at the elevator. Blake pressed the down button. "They're warm and friendly," he added. Blake shrugged her shoulders. Bassem put his index finger under her chin and tilted her head. He searched her eyes before he pressed a small kiss against her lips.

"I want to take you out for dinner," he said to her.

"You do?" Blake asked. Bassem nodded. "Then take me out."

Bassem smiled. "I will pick you up tomorrow. We have much to talk about," he said. Blake frowned a little.

"That is not usually a good thing," she said. Bassem smiled.

"Don't worry, it'll be good. I just think you need to know everything about me before we move forward." He leaned closer to her and kissed her lips again.

Blake watched Bassem walking into the elevator. Her heart was beating fast. She touched her red cheeks. He made her so shy. But what did he mean when he said going forward? What was forward? He needed to be clear. Were they going to have a professional relationship or did he want to be her boyfriend? And what was it that he wanted to tell her? What did she need to know?

***

The next day, Aunt Moira helped Blake find something to wear for her date with Bassem. "You want to look sexy and sophisticated," she said to Blake.

"What about these trousers?" she asked her aunt.

"You can't wear trousers on a date with a sheikh."

Blake shrugged her shoulders. CJ and her mother burst into laughter. "Seriously Blake," said CJ as she shook her head.

"I've been with a rich man before." said Aunt Moira. "Trust me on this." She pulled out a royal blue dress with a boat neck from the closet.

"That is a gorgeous dress," said Blake's mother. Blake went into the bathroom and put on the dress.

"Wow Blake," CJ said as she walked back into the room. The dress hugged her curves and complemented her figure.

"I have some pearls to go with the dress," said Aunt Moira. She fished some out of her bag and put them on Blake.

"You walk around with a pearl necklace in your bag?" Blake asked her.

"I am always prepared."

They all burst into laughter. Blake finished off her outfit with a pair of high heels. She left her hair untied, then put on red lipstick. Just when Blake sprayed on some perfume, the doorbell sounded.

"I will see you all later," she said to them and rushed for the door. She opened the door, and there was her Adonis. Bassem stood at the door. He looked at Blake slowly from head to toe.

"You look gorgeous," he said to her.

"I'm glad you think so." Blake smiled. She tried to play it cool but inside she was melting.

Chapter 21

Bassem and Blake arrived at a five-star restaurant. Bassem had picked the finest restaurant in Austin. He wanted only the finest for Blake. It had taken him a while to come to terms with his feelings for her. When his brother had said that he would make a move on her, the thought of it infuriated him. He couldn't handle the thought of her being with another man.

When she stormed into his office and confronted him about kissing her and then ignoring her afterwards, he found it both amusing and adorable. If only she knew that he had been struggling too. He wanted to kiss her also. He didn't like seeing *Lenny* flirting with her. He wanted to rip his hand off every time he touched Blake.

"There is no one here," Blake pointed out as the waiter escorted them to their table.

"I had the place closed down," said Bassem, hoping that Blake would find it impressive.

"You did?" Her eyes widened. "You have to book at least two months in advance just to get a table here, and you closed it down?" she added.

"Yes." Bassem grinned at her.

He pulled out the chair for her. Blake smiled at him as she sat down. Bassem was going out of his way to impress Blake. He had never done that for any woman before. He tucked her in and then went to sit opposite her. The waiter gave them their menus.

"Oh!" Blake cried out when she saw the menu. "So expensive," she whispered.

"Order whatever you like," he said to her. She put her menu down.

"You can order for me," she said. "The food doesn't matter. I'm just very curious about what you want to say to me."

Bassem nodded. He called the waiter over and gave him their orders. He turned his attention to the beautiful woman sitting across from him. The dress she wore complemented her figure and her complexion. Bassem couldn't keep his eyes off her. He cleared his throat.

"Am I right to assume that you are completely single?" he asked her.

"Yes," Blake replied.

"Good because I don't like sharing."

Blake smiled. "You don't ever have to worry about that," she said to him. The waiter came over with their drinks.

"You need to find someone to replace Leonard," he said before he took a sip of his drink. Blake raised her eyebrows.

"Lenny? Why? He's doing a good job," she replied.

"I don't like how he looks at you and takes every chance he gets to touch you."

"What?" Blake started laughing.

"I am serious."

"You are overreacting."

"Am I?"

"Yes, you are."

Bassem frowned and looked away. He didn't like that man and he was never going to like him. The waiter brought their food and then disappeared back to the kitchen.

"Are you single?" Blake asked him.

"Am I?" Bassem needed to tell her about Keira but he didn't want Blake to leave him.

"You're a handsome and healthy young man. You'd probably have someone."

"I don't."

"Oh." Blake looked at her food and attempted to hide her smile but Bassem saw it.

"I am engaged," he said. Blake looked up so fast.

"What?" she spat out. He explained to her that his parents wanted him to marry Keira and that the marriage was to take place in two months.

"I feel sick." Blake put her fork down.

"I don't have any feelings for her," he said.

"That doesn't make me feel better."

Bassem fished a black velvet box out of his pocket and put it on the table. Blake looked at it and then at him with a questioning gaze. "Open it," he said to her.

"Why? What is it?" Blake took the box and opened it. She gasped at the sight of the large diamond ring. She looked at him for an explanation.

"I want to marry you and not her," he said to her.

"Ay." Blake rubbed the temples of her head. "You have a very odd way of doing things."

Bassem couldn't disagree with that. "I wanted to propose to you first before I told my parents that I didn't want to marry her," he said to her. Blake was silent for a moment. She looked as though she was thinking.

"Why do you want to marry me?" she asked him.

"You're the only woman I've ever thought about as much as I do. You're smart and beautiful. When my brother was kidnapped, you were there for me. You stayed by my side and came with me to look for my brother. Not many women would do that," he explained.

"Do you have feelings for me?"

"Yes. As much as I tried to deny them, they only grew stronger."

She was silent for a moment. Then she picked up her fork. "I'm going to finish up my food because it looks too good to leave," she said to him. Bassem smiled and shook his head.

"How do you feel about me?" he asked her.

"Um." The question clearly caught Blake off guard. Bassem watched her cheeks turn red. "I'm in love with you and that scares me," she said. She was too scared to look at him.

"Look at me," he demanded. Blake looked at him. "Why does it scare you?"

"I haven't known you for that long. How do I know that you won't break my heart?"

"You've seen how I am. I'm more into my work than women. I will never betray you."

"Marrying you means that I'll be the queen of Al Huddah. Oh lord." She looked nervous.

"Yes."

"I'm not qualified enough. I know nothing about your culture."

"You will learn."

Blake gave him a nervous smile. "Well, I won't give you an answer until this other woman is out of the picture," she said.

"That is fair enough." Bassem understood that she wanted to marry him also but wanted Keira out of the picture. He knew that he had to go back to Al Huddah and talk to his parents. It was not going to be easy but he had to do it.

***

"Are you ready?" Basil asked Bassem.

"No, but it has to be done." Bassem had returned with Basil to Al Huddah. He had to tell his parents about Blake, and Basil had offered his support.

The two brothers walked into the king's living room. Their father was sitting at the sofas with his wife. "What are the two of you doing here?" the king asked. He looked so surprised to see his sons. Bassem and Basil bowed their heads to their father.

"It's so nice to see you twice in a month," said the queen.

"Have a seat," the king said to them. Bassem bowed his head.

"I cannot obey your command." He went straight to the point. There was no need to make small talk.

"What are you talking about?"

"I can't marry Keira."

The queen gasped and placed her hand on her heart. "But she is a great girl," she said.

"You found her to be unsuitable?" the king asked.

"It's not that." Bassem cleared his throat. "I wish to marry someone else."

The queen raised her eyebrows. "The woman Basil mentioned before?" she asked.

"Yes," Bassem replied.

"Is she Arabic?" the king asked calmly.

"No."

"Then no. I will not approve that marriage."

"I told you before. She has to be Arabic," said the queen. She shook her head.

"She is a great woman. You will love her," said Basil.

"Did you introduce her to him?"

"He had nothing to do with this," said Bassem.

"We can't have the queen of Al Huddah not Arabic. Does that even make sense?" said the queen.

"If I have to marry, it has to be her," said Bassem. The king and the queen looked at each other.

"You are trying my patience," said the king.

"I'm sorry, Father, but I love this woman and I can't imagine marrying someone else."

The king picked up a cup and threw it at Bassem. Basil and the queen gasped at the same time. "Is a woman worth you disobeying me?" he shouted.

"Father, please calm down," said Basil.

"Is she pregnant?"

"I've never slept with her," said Bassem. The king rubbed the temples of his head.

"That is what has gotten you this stupid?"

"Okay, why don't you marry Keira and then have this woman as a concubine?" the queen suggested. Basil and Bassem both looked at her as though she had lost her mind. "It's common for kings to have concubines," she added.

"I only want her," said Bassem.

"A Western woman cannot be the queen," said the king.

"I will give up the throne," said Bassem. Basil whipped his head in Bassem's direction.

"What?" he spat out.

"He's gone mad," said the king. Bassem bowed his head to the king and walked out of the room.

Chapter 22

Tara knocked on Blake's office door. "There is someone here to see you," she said.

"Who?" Blake asked.

"Me," a tall, middle-aged woman said as she walked into her office. The woman wore a navy blue dress and beautiful expensive jewelry. She looked so elegant and beautiful.

"Good afternoon, ma'am," Blake greeted her. She nodded at Tara. The receptionist smiled and walked out of the office. "Would you like to have a seat?"

"Yes." The woman sat down at Blake's desk. Blake didn't recognize her but didn't want to be rude to her since she was older. So she didn't ask who she was.

"How may I help you today?" she asked her.

"I'm Bassem's mother."

Blake gasped loudly. She quickly sprung up to her feet. "Your majesty." She bowed her head.

"Have a seat," the queen said to her. Blake nodded and sat down. "I wanted to see the woman that made my son lose his mind."

"I don't follow."

"He told us that he wishes to marry you. A Westerner." She didn't look pleased at all. Bassem had gone to Al Huddah after he proposed to her but when he returned, he just told her that he broke it off with Keira and had told his parents that he wanted to marry Blake.

"Yes, the sheikh and I have been talking about marriage." Blake had told her parents and Aunt Moira that the sheikh wanted to marry her. Her mother and aunt were happy about it. They had fallen for Bassem from the first time they had met him.

"This marriage cannot happen," said the queen.

"Why not?"

"My son needs to marry an Arabic woman."

It broke Blake's heart to know that his mother didn't want her to marry Bassem just because she wasn't Arabic. "I know that I'm not Arabic but I will do whatever it takes to be a good wife. I really love Bassem," she said.

"Love means nothing. My son is willing to give up the throne for you," said the queen. Blake gasped.

"He never told me that."

The queen raised an eyebrow. "You're telling me that you didn't know about this?" she asked.

"No."

"You didn't put him up to this?"

"No, I'd never do such a thing."

"I've been watching you. I know that you are a good girl and you've never been with many men," she said. Blake raised her eyebrows. The queen had looked into her.

"You've looked into me?" she asked.

"Of course. I need to know about the people my son associates with."

"I see."

"I have nothing against you. It's just that you're not Arabic."

That didn't make Blake feel better. She couldn't change herself and be Arabic. "That shouldn't matter," she said.

"He is not an ordinary man. He is the crown prince of Al Huddah, of course it matters."

"If you need me to learn the language and the culture, I am willing to do so." She was willing to learn all she needed but she was nervous about becoming a queen. That came with so much responsibility. It scared her but as long as Bassem was at her side, she could do anything.

"What if you come to live at the palace and serve my son in private?"

Blake's eyes widened. "Like a concubine?" she asked.

"Yes." The queen nodded. She was suggesting something so absurd but managed to still look and sound elegant.

"I'm sorry, I couldn't do that," said Blake. "If he is willing to marry someone else, then I would have to let him go. I can't be his concubine. I'm not with him for money, power or sex. I genuinely love him."

The queen was silent for a moment. "Can you come with me?" she said to Blake as she rose to her feet.

"Where are we going?" Blake stood up.

"To see my son."

"Okay."

Blake and the queen headed out of Blake's office. "If Michaela looks for me, tell her I'm out with Sheikh Sedarous's mother," she said to Tara.

"Okay." Tara smiled and nodded.

***

The ride to Bassem's office was pretty awkward for Blake. The queen asked her a lot of questions. It was clear that she was trying to get a feel for the kind of woman Blake was. At one point, she was on the phone speaking in Arabic.

They arrived at Bassem's building moments later. They got into the elevator and headed to Bassem's office. The sheikh was sitting at his desk looking at some paperwork. His eyes widened when he saw Blake and his mother walking into his office.

"What in the world?" He rose to his feet. "Why are the two of you together?"

"I wanted to see the woman that managed to get your heart," said the queen. Bassem walked around his desk and kissed his mother on the cheek. Then he held Blake by her waist and pressed a small gentle kiss against her lips.

"I see," Bassem replied. The queen walked over to the sofas in his office and sat down. "Did she yell at you?" Bassem whispered in Blake's ear.

"No," Blake replied. "But you are willing to give up the throne for me?" she whispered.

"She told you that?"

"Yes. Why would you do that? I never asked you to do that."

"Stop whispering and come over here," said the queen. Blake looked at Bassem and mouthed *this conversation is not over*. She wanted to marry Bassem but not like that. She didn't want him to give up anything to be with her.

They both went to join his mother at the sofas.

"I spoke to your father a few minutes ago," said the queen.

"About what?" Bassem asked.

"About this situation."

"And what did he say?"

The queen sighed heavily. "We looked into Blake. She has a clean record. She's never done any questionable acts. She won't bring shame to our family," she said.

"What are you saying to me right now?" Bassem asked.

"If you give up the throne, it means that Basil will be the king. Your father doesn't want that. Your brother is too immature and knows nothing about running a country."

"He can learn."

The queen shook her head. "He doesn't want to be the king either. He spent his entire life not wanting the position," she said to him.

"So what will happen now?" Bassem asked. The queen sighed again.

"We have no choice but to let you marry her." She looked at Blake. Bassem and Blake gasped and looked at each other.

"You mean that?" Bassem asked his mother.

"I don't make jokes."

"You can't take it back!"

"It's your father's orders." She rose to her feet. Bassem quickly got up and kissed his mother on the cheek.

"Thank you," he said to her. Blake stood up and bowed her head to his mother.

"Thank you so much," she said.

"Just don't make me regret it." With that, the queen walked out of the office. Bassem picked Blake up into his arms and spun around.

"This is good! I'm so happy," he said. He held Blake tightly and kissed her. Blake hit him playfully.

"You should have told me that that was how your parents felt," she said.

"I didn't want it to upset you."

"No more secrets, no matter what."

"Sure." Bassem kissed Blake again. Blake had gone through so many emotions in one day. She was just glad that she was going to marry the man she loved more than anything.

"You know, you'll have to give me many children," said Bassem. Blake wrapped her arms around his neck.

"How many?" she asked.

"Four or five."

"What? No, that's not happening. Two children are enough."

"I want one son as my heir and three girls that look just like you."

Blake rolled her eyes and smiled. "I want a boy just like you," she said.

"I love you," Bassem said to her.

"I love you too," Blake replied and kissed him.

"The pair of you are so cheesy," Basil said as he walked into the office. Bassem put Blake down.

"Congratulations, I just saw mother on the way out," Basil said. He leaned in to kiss Blake on the cheek but Bassem stopped him.

"No more of that," said Bassem. Basil laughed.

"I've never had feelings for her. I was always trying to get you to admit yours, that's it."

Blake smiled. "It's your turn to find a wife," she said to him.

"Not anytime soon."

The three of them laughed and hugged each other. Blake was perfectly happy. The happiest she had ever been in her life.

What to read next?

If you liked this book, you will also like *In Love with a Haunted House*. Another interesting book is *The Oil Prince*.

In Love With a Haunted House

The last thing Mallory Clark wants to do is move back home. She has no choice, though, since the company she worked for in Chicago has just downsized her, and everybody else. To make matters worse her fiancé has broken their engagement, and her heart, leaving her hurting and scarred. When her mother tells her that the house she always coveted as a child, the once-famed Gray Oaks Manor, is not only on the market but selling for a song, it seems to Mallory that the best thing she could possibly do would be to put Chicago, and everything and everyone in it, behind her. Arriving back home she runs into gorgeous and mysterious Blake Hunter. Blake is new to town and like her he is interested in buying the crumbling old Victorian on the edge of the historic downtown center, although his reasons are his own. Blake is instantly intrigued by the flame-haired beauty with the fiery temper and the vulnerable expression in her eyes. He can feel the attraction between them and knows it is mutual, but he also knows that the last thing on earth he needs is to get involved with a woman determined to take away a house he has to have.

The Oil Prince

A car drives over a puddle and muddy water splashes Emily, who was just out for a walk, from head to toe. When she sees the car parked at a gas station moments later, she decides to confront the man leaning against it. The handsome man refuses to apologize, and after hearing what Emily thinks about him, watches her leave. The next day, fate plays a joke on Emily when she finds out that the man is her boss's brother and a prince of a Middle Eastern country. Prince Basil often appears in tabloids because of different scandals and in order to tame his temper, his father sends him to work on a project of drilling a methane well in Dallas. If Basil refuses or is unsuccessful, his financial accounts will be blocked and his title of prince will be revoked. Although their characters clash, Emily and Basil fall in love while working together and Basil's heart melts. When the project that can significantly improve his family business hits a major obstacle, Basil proves that love has tremendous power and shows a side of himself that nobody knew existed.

About Kate Goldman

In childhood I observed a huge love between my mother and father and promised myself that one day I would meet a man whom I would fall in love with head over heels. At the age of 16, I wrote my first romance story that was published in a student magazine and was read by my entire neighborhood. I enjoy writing romance stories that readers can turn into captivating imaginary movies where characters fall in love, overcome difficult obstacles, and participate in best adventures of their lives. Most of the time you can find me reading a great fiction book in a cozy armchair, writing a romance story in a hammock near the ocean, or traveling around the world with my beloved husband.

One Last Thing…

If you believe that *The Twin Sheikhs* is worth sharing, would you spend a minute to let your friends know about it?

If this book lets them have a great time, they will be enormously grateful to you – as will I.

Kate

www.KateGoldmanBooks.com

Printed in Great Britain
by Amazon